THE MULLIGAN CHRONICLES

Second Chances

A Story of Loss, Faith, and Redemption

by Martin Thompson

Martin Thompson Books · Fort Worth, Texas

Copyright © 2026 Martin Thompson. All rights reserved.

No part of this book may be reproduced, stored in a retrieval system, or transmitted in any form or by any means—electronic, mechanical, photocopying, recording, or otherwise—without the prior written permission of the author, except for brief quotations used in reviews or other noncommercial uses permitted by copyright law.

This is a work of fiction. Names, characters, places, and incidents are either the product of the author's imagination or are used fictitiously. Any resemblance to actual persons, living or dead, or to actual events is purely coincidental.

ISBN 979-8-9944220-6-4 (paperback)

ISBN 979-8-9944220-7-1 (hardcover)

ISBN 979-8-9944220-8-8 (ebook)

Published in 2026 by Martin Thompson Books

Fort Worth, Texas

Printed in the United States of America

Dedication

For **Janice**,

my partner in every good story.

For **Jon, Palmer, and Olivia**,

who carry the family name — and the flame.

For **Fawn and Myrl Furry**,

the finest in-laws a man could ask for.

For **Phil Cloud**,

whom I will always remember as a brother.

And for every family I've had the honor to serve —

This one's for you.

Author's Note

Every good story begins with a question.

This one began with a sign.

TALKING DOG — $20.

I've spent my life in a profession that trains you to be observant, calm, and skeptical in equal measure. Funeral directors are not, by nature, gullible people. Still, curiosity has always been one of my weaknesses, and on that afternoon, it got the better of me.

What follows is not a book about whether dogs can talk. It's a book about what happens when grief, love, faith, and humor collide in a life already full of stories. Some details are exaggerated. Some are borrowed. A few are truer than I ever expected when I first wrote them down.

This is a work of fiction—but it is rooted in real places, real people, and real moments of kindness, loss, and laughter. If you're looking for realism, you'll find it. If you're looking for plausibility, I make no guarantees.

I only ask that you read with an open mind, a forgiving heart, and a willingness to believe that sometimes the most important voices in our lives arrive from unexpected places—and occasionally on four legs.

This story has been told before with a lighter step and a louder laugh.

That version leaned into humor first — because sometimes laughter is how we survive what hurts.

This version leans more deeply into the heart of the journey. Into grief, faith, friendship, and the quiet ways healing finds us when we're not looking for it.

The humor is still here. It always will be. But in this telling, it serves the story rather than leading it.

Preface

For nearly fifty years, I've stood beside families at some of their most difficult moments. I've watched grief enter rooms quietly and leave them changed. I've also learned that even in the heaviest hours, laughter has a way of sneaking in—often when it's least expected and most needed.

This story grew out of that space.

Talking Dog $20 is about second chances—some earned, some accidental, and some delivered with a wagging tail and a list of demands. It's about the strange grace that shows up when life stops making sense and insists on being lived anyway. Along the way, it touches on faith, friendship, marriage, memory, and the peculiar ways love insists on rearranging our plans.

At its heart, this is a story about listening—listening to people, to silence, and sometimes to voices we'd rather dismiss as impossible. Because occasionally, the thing that sounds the most unbelievable is the very thing we need to hear.

If this book makes you laugh, I'm glad.

If it makes you pause, I'm grateful.

And if it reminds you of someone—human or otherwise—who changed your life simply by showing up, then it has done its job.

— Martin Thompson

Fort Worth, Texas

Table of Contents

Dedication iv

Author's Note v

Preface vii

Table of Contents viii

Chapter 1 — Talking Dog, $20 2

Chapter 2 — Before Mulligan (The Week the Laughter Died) 8

Chapter 3 — Mulligan Moves In 14

Chapter 4 — Mulligan at the Funeral Home 20

Chapter 5 — The Whole Story 26

Chapter 6 — Julia's Pack 32

Chapter 7 — My Story 40

Chapter 8 — The Lady in White 46

Chapter 9 — Fetch, Fatso, Fetch 50

Chapter 10 — The Adoption 56

Chapter 11 — The Comfort Dog Team 62

Chapter 12 — The Family from Monterrey 68

Chapter 13 — Father Ben and the Choir 74

Chapter 14 — The Funeral Mass 80

Chapter 15 — Movie Night Revival 86

Chapter 16 — Family Night 92

Chapter 17 — Night at the Club (The Men of Mitzvah) .. 98

Chapter 18 — Marketing Mayhem 104

Chapter 19 — A Visit to Remember 110

Chapter 20 — The Golf Club Incident 114

Chapter 21 — Back to the Beginning 120

Chapter 22 — The Pawdcast 126

Chapter 23 — Sunny Day 134

Chapter 24 — Sunny's Funeral 140

Chapter 25 — One More Hole -in -One 148

Chapter 26 — America's Team, Heaven's Wish 154

Chapter 27 — The Blessing of the Beasts (and Everything Else) 160

Chapter 28 — Back to Santa Anna 166

Chapter 29 — Back Among the Living 172

Chapter 30 — After the Storm 176

Acknowledgments 180

About the Author 181

Chapter 1 — Talking Dog, $20

You've probably heard this one.

But not the way I tell it.

Picture a man driving down a road one afternoon when he spots a hand-painted sign that reads:

TALKING DOG — $20

He laughs.

No way.

Still, curiosity gets the better of him. He pulls over, walks up to the porch, and knocks on the door.

A man answers.

"I'm here about the talking dog," the man says.

The owner nods, as if this happens all the time. "Come on in."

They sit down in the living room. The owner calls out, "Fred!"

In trots a golden retriever.

The owner gestures toward him. "Go ahead," he says. "Do your deal."

Fred sits, clears his throat, and says,

"Hi. I'm Fred. I'm a talking dog."

The man nearly falls out of his chair. "That's incredible!" he says. "What's your story?"

Fred stretches his paws and launches in like he's giving a TED Talk.

"When I was a pup," "I was owned by a bad guy named Jefe. He figured out quickly what I could do, so he'd have me sit in in meetings and tell him who was stealing his money, who was skimming from the drug stash, and who might be about to put a hit on him.

"It wasn't all bad — soft bed, good food, and good dog treats. Then one day, this beautiful Golden Doodle named Matilda came trotting by. We fell in love, got married, and she started training to be a therapy and show dog. Matilda decided my line of work was too dangerous and told me to find something safer.

"So, I switched sides — worked for the police department, then the FBI, and finally the CIA. We solved crimes, stopped bad guys, and I even broke up a terrorist plot once. After all that, Matilda said, 'Fred, you really need a safer job.'

"So, I became a dog trainer. Since I speak both Dog and Human, I can train faster than anyone else. That's my story."

The man sits there stunned.

Finally, he turns to the owner and asks, "Why in the world are you selling this dog for twenty dollars?"

The owner shrugs.

"Because he's a liar. He made every bit of that up."

That's the joke.

That's how it always ends.

I've told it hundreds of times — at Chamber meetings, Optimist Club luncheons, funeral conventions, even a few pulpits when the preacher didn't mind a little laughter before the sermon.

People laugh every time.

And every time they do, I think the same thing:

What if the man bought the dog?

That's where this story begins.

It was a blistering afternoon in Texas — the kind that melts the chrome off a hearse.

I'd just finished a graveside service where a gust of wind knocked over half the flower stands and sent one poor lady sprinting from a fire-ant mound like she was reenacting the Book of Revelation.

I was headed back to the funeral home when I saw it.

A hand-painted sign on a crooked post:

TALKING DOG — $20

I laughed.

About a hundred yards later, I slowed down.

Curiosity has a way of doing that — tapping you on the shoulder just when you think you're done for the day.

I pulled over.

The fella who answered the door wore a stained T-shirt, a World's Best Grandpa cap, and the calm confidence of a man who'd already lived through the punchline.

"I'm here about your talking dog," I said.

"Come on in," he replied.

He called out, "Mulligan!"

Out trotted a scruffy mutt — fur sticking every direction, one ear up and one ear giving up on the day, eyes the color of strong coffee. He looked less like a pedigree and more like a pile of borrowed parts from the shelter.

He sat right in front of me, tilted his head, and said — clear as a bell —

"Hi. I'm Mulligan. And I'm a talking dog."

My knees nearly buckled.

His voice wasn't forced or barky. It was smooth. Confident. A little smug.

But it was his eyes that got me — kind eyes, smart eyes, eyes that looked like they'd seen loss and decided to keep going anyway.

"What's your story?" I asked.

He perked up, his tail sweeping the floor.

"You wouldn't believe it if I told you, "He said — and smiled.

"When I was a pup," he began, "I belonged to a bad guy named Jefe. Mean fella. It smelled like cheap tequila and worse decisions. He figured out early that I could talk, so he used me to listen to his friends, who were stealing, who were plotting, who were about to get whacked.

"It wasn't all bad. Soft bed, prime-rib scraps, and chew toys that used to belong to people who crossed him."

He paused, eyes narrowing like he was remembering.

"Then one day, this beautiful Standard Poodle named Georgette came trotting by — white as snow, walked like she'd been to finishing school in Paris. She was training to be a therapy and show dog and told me straight up, 'Mulligan, you're wasting your life working for thugs. You've got a gift.'

"Well, when a lady like that gives you career advice, you listen. I switched sides — helped the police, then the FBI, and eventually the CIA. I sniffed out smugglers, foiled a few bad guys, and once accidentally bit a senator. Long story. Classified.

"After all that, Georgette said I needed something safer. So, I became a dog trainer. Since I speak both Dog and Human, I can train faster than any person alive. That's my story."

I blinked. "You're serious?"

He nodded once, wagging his tail. "Every word of it."

I turned to the owner. "Why in the world are you selling this dog for twenty dollars?"

The man shrugged.

"Because he's a liar. He made every bit of that up."

Mulligan's ears flattened.

"Hey," he said, "maybe a little embellished. But the Georgette part's true."

And for reasons I still can't explain, I believed him.

Maybe it was exhaustion.

Maybe it was faith disguised as foolishness.

But I reached into my wallet, handed the man a twenty-dollar bill, and said, "I'll take him."

The man nodded. "You won't regret it."

Mulligan hopped into my passenger seat like he'd been waiting for his whole life for that moment. He smelled faintly of dust, bacon, and something familiar — that same mix of grass and shampoo that used to cling to our old cocker spaniel, Charlie, after a day at the ranch.

The sun hung low. The highway shimmered.

And that scruffy mutt sat tall beside me, tongue out, eyes forward, like we'd been partners forever.

For twenty bucks, I thought I was buying a laugh.

Turns out, I was buying a miracle — one that would change everything I thought I knew about love, loss, and the strange mercy of second chances.

Because sometimes miracles don't ride in on clouds.

Sometimes they smell like corn chips, and shed on your seat,

and cost twenty dollars.

Chapter 2 — Before Mulligan (The Week the Laughter Died)

The funny thing about miracles is that they don't wait for you to be ready. They show up when the laughter's gone quiet and the house feels one sigh away from breaking.

That's where we were when Mulligan came along.

Julia's daddy, Burl Martin, was one of those small -but -mighty Texans who could outwork men half his age and knew every cow by number and temperament. He ran a cow-calf ranch outside Santa Anna, red-dirt country where the horizon rolls like a slow tide. On the side, he kept a few old stripper wells, coaxing oil out of the ground one stubborn gallon at a time.

It wasn't wealth, but it was honest, and Burl loved every sun-burned minute of it.

He loved his daughter more.

When I married Julia, Burl and her mama, Dane, didn't just welcome me — they drafted me. Burl and I bonded quickly over sports. We talked every day: Rangers baseball, Cowboys football, Mavericks basketball — arguing over bad coaching and laughing about worse luck.

He treated my boy, Clint, like the grandson he never stopped bragging about. We weren't blood, but it never mattered.

Then came the call.

Burl had fallen at the post office — hit his head on the steps. By the time we reached the hospital, machines were doing the breathing.

Within hours, he was gone.

The silence in that waiting room was the kind that rearranges your insides.

Back home, our three dogs — Anna Belle, Teddy, and Charlie — kept orbiting around Julia like confused satellites.

Charlie was her shadow. A black cocker spaniel, loyal as sunrise and spoiled as a grandchild. He'd curl in her lap, follow her everywhere, and somehow knew when we hit the outskirts of Dublin, Texas — home of the old-fashioned Dr Pepper bottling plant. His tail would start thumping before we even saw the sign.

We'd pull in for three frosty cups — one for Julia, one for me, one for him. He'd gulp his down in one heroic slurp and finish with a burp that rattled the dashboard.

Julia laughed every single time.

That week, laughter left the building.

Three days after Burl's funeral, Charlie collapsed in her lap. By Friday, he was gone too.

Two losses in one week — the man who'd raised her and the dog who'd loved her like a child.

You could almost hear the hinge of her heart creak shut.

Through it all, Dane stood steady — small, silver-haired, every inch a Texas lady. She could feed ten people on nothing but flour and faith, and she never needed to tell you she was praying for you; you could feel it in the room.

After Burl passed, she tried to stay at the ranch awhile, but the silence out there was too much.

So, she moved in with us.

Every morning, she sits at the breakfast table with her Bible and a pen, underlining verses like she's afraid the ink might run out before she does. At ninety-six, I'm honestly amazed there's a verse left untouched. Some mornings, I think she's down to highlighting the page numbers.

She'll look up and say something like, "The Lord's carried heavier loads, honey."

And she's right.

But even miracles like Dane need company.

By then, I'd been in the funeral business for fifty years — the first twenty-two under my dad, then out on my own. I'd built a thriving firm in Grapevine, lost it to a bad partnership that nearly wiped us out, then clawed my way back.

My son, Clint, and I came back to Fort Worth to start again. We opened Cole Sheridan & Son Funeral Home: honest prices, genuine compassion, no marble chandeliers needed to prove we cared.

Five years before that crooked roadside sign, my siblings called. A hospital wanted to buy our family's old funeral home property — Guy Sheridan Funeral Home, the one my father poured his life into. My siblings offered to sell us the business, and if Clint and I wanted it, we could buy it — but we'd have thirty days to move it.

So, we did what Sheridan's do: we said yes first and figured out the impossible second.

We found an old church nobody wanted — peeling paint, pigeons in the rafters, and more potential than good sense. While the world shut down for COVID, we remodeled every inch: a stained-glass chapel, a new reception hall, and a parking lot that could fit a small parade.

We poured our savings and our souls into it.

And when it opened, it was beautiful.

Still is.

But families are creatures of habit, and our old ones followed the highway to newer zip codes. We were serving new people — grateful people — but the familiar names, the ones that built us, had drifted away.

Most nights, I'd stay after everyone left, lights off, just the glow from the stained glass on my father's old portrait. I'd sit there wondering if I'd made the right choices — or if I'd used up whatever luck God had given me.

At home, Julia moved through the rooms as if she feared waking memories. Anna Belle and Teddy stayed close but couldn't fill the space Charlie left.

At night, Anna Belle would snuggle next to Julia in bed like Charlie once had. Julia's hand would find its way to that warm little head, and that was enough to make it through till morning. Dane kept the coffee hot and the faith steady, but even she looked smaller under that big kitchen light.

Grief had settled in like an unwanted roommate.

One night, I whispered to myself, "Maybe I'm just tired."

Maybe I was.

That was the state of things — Julia's silence, Dane's scriptures, my exhaustion, and a house that had forgotten how to laugh — when, on one hot Texas afternoon, heading home from another graveside service, I saw it.

A hand-painted sign on a crooked post.

TALKING DOG — $20.

I laughed — the kind of half-laugh you make when your heart's still broken, but you're not ready to quit trying.

Then I hit the brakes.

Because sometimes hope doesn't look like an angel or a burning bush.

Sometimes it just looks like a crooked sign at the edge of a dusty road.

Chapter 3 — Mulligan Moves In

By the time I pulled into the driveway, the sun was sliding down behind the big pecan tree, and the dashboard thermometer said we were just a few degrees shy of boiling coffee. Mulligan had his head halfway out the window, tongue flapping, tail keeping time with the wind. He looked perfectly content — like a hitchhiker who'd finally found the right ride.

Julia stood on the porch, arms folded in that way that says, whatever's in that Suburban, it's not staying.

"Don't be mad," I said as I got out.

"Why would I be mad?" she asked — every husband knows that's not an honest question.

Then she saw him.

Her eyebrows climbed. "Cole Sheridan, what on earth is that?"

"That," I said proudly, "is Mulligan."

"You named him already?"

"He came pre-named. Like a clearance item."

She stared at the scruffy mutt — fur in every direction, one ear standing tall, one giving up on the day. "He looks like he fell through a brush pile."

"He's got character."

"Character smells like dirt."

"Nothing a bath and some love can't fix."

Mulligan trotted up the steps, tail swinging like he owned the place. He stopped in front of Julia, sat, and offered a polite nod.

"Why did you buy this dog?" she asked.

"Well," I said, scratching my neck, "he talks."

Her look said, you've finally cracked.

"Just… watch," I said.

Mulligan sighed, straightened, and said — clear as a bell —

"Evening, ma'am. I'm Mulligan. Emotional support, part-time philosopher, and — depending on the kitchen schedule — a food critic in training."

Julia froze.

"Cole Sheridan," she said slowly, "that dog just talked."

"Told you."

She sat down carefully, as if afraid she might spook the miracle. "All right, Mulligan," she said. "What's your story?"

Mulligan crossed his front paws like a man settling in to tell it right.

"Well," he began, "when I was a pup, I belonged to a fella named Jefe. Good name. Bad choices. He was in what you might call the import-export business. He liked having me sit in meetings because I don't gossip, and I never forget. It worked fine until he realized I was smarter than half his crew. That got awkward. So, one night, I grabbed a biscuit and went AWOL.

"I wandered for a while — sleeping behind dumpsters, stealing sandwiches from delivery drivers. Nothing I'm proud of. Then, on a rainy night, I ended up at the Presbyterian Night Shelter downtown. They took me in. No questions. No collar check. Just, 'Here's a blanket, boy.'

"I moved into the women's center. Those women had all faced difficult circumstances—some were escaping dangerous men; others were fleeing misfortune—but every one of them longed to be acknowledged. So, I made my rounds each night. A nudge here. A paw there. One little boy told me I smelled like safety, which, I admit, was mostly shampoo and Fritos."

He paused.

"It was the best job I ever had — until one of the staff decided he could sell me. He 're-homed' me without permission. Sold me for fifty bucks and a set of used tires. Can you imagine? Traded a miracle for Firestones."

Julia's hand went to her mouth — half shocking, half holding back a laugh.

"Did you ever find him?" she asked.

"Ma'am," Mulligan said, "I'm working on forgiveness. But if I ever do, I'll forgive him after I bite his ass."

From behind us, Dane appeared in her housecoat, Bible in one hand, coffee in the other. She'd been watching from the doorway, curiosity twinkling in eyes that had seen nearly a century of everything.

"Oh my," she said, "a talking dog."

Mulligan turned toward her and gave a respectful bow. "Evening, ma'am. You must be the prayer department."

"That I am."

"Well," he said, "I may need a little extra coverage. I've had experiences."

Dane chuckled, shaking her head. "Lord help us, I believe you have."

Julia leaned back in her chair, studying him — the shape of his head, the way he rested his paw on her foot without thinking. She didn't say it, but I could see it in her eyes. He reminded her of Charlie — the same gentle stillness, the same sense that he knew things without being told.

Teddy circled Mulligan like he was inspecting new inventory. You could almost see him thinking, Another stray? Anna Belle took a different approach. She offered a sniff and a sigh, then promptly sat beside Julia, tail tucked — her opinion delivered without a word.

Julia leaned against the counter and opened a cold Dr Pepper, one of her small rituals. She took a sip, still watching him.

"Well," she said, "you've certainly had quite a life."

"Ma'am," Mulligan replied, "every life's quite a life when you're paying attention."

She smiled at that — her first easy smile in months.

He watched the can fizz in her hand and added, "I love Dr Pepper. You got another?"

Julia laughed — a real laugh, the kind that starts low and surprises even the person making it. Even Anna Belle's tail joined in, thumping softly like an amen.

"Cole," she said, "get this dog a Dr Pepper."

I grinned. "I think he's already saving us money on therapy."

Mulligan wagged once, slow, and sure. "Ma'am, I'm just getting started."

That night, the house felt lighter.

Not loud.

Not healed.

Just lighter.

And after months of silence, that was plenty.

Chapter 4 — Mulligan at the Funeral Home

Morning sunlight slid through the stained-glass windows of Guy Sheridan Funeral Home, scattering color across the carpet like somebody had spilled grace all over the floor.
I pushed the front door open and held it for Mulligan.

"Big day," I told him. "First impressions count."

He gave a slow wag. "I prefer lasting ones."

Inside, the crew looked up from their usual rhythm — coffee cups, clipboards, quiet talk.
They all froze for half a beat, then relaxed, because after all these years, nothing I bring through that door surprises them anymore.

Fa was first. She peeked over her glasses, the way she does when she's deciding whether to scold or smile. "Cole, who's this handsome devil?"

"This," I said, "is Mulligan. He's joining the team."

She crouched to eye level. "Well, aren't you something? Adorably ugly, but adorable just the same. Lord, you need a bath."

"Ma'am," Mulligan said under his breath, "morale before hygiene."

Fa blinked. "Did he just—"
"Not yet," I said quickly. "We'll get to that."

Larry waddled out from the prep-room doorway, coffee in hand, grin already working overtime. "Good grief, boss. He's uglier than me."

"That's debatable," I said.

Larry looked Mulligan up and down. "Are you sure that thing's even housebroken?"
"He's not a thing," I said. "He's our new *Emotional Support Dog*."

The room went quiet.

"Everybody grab a seat," I said, motioning toward the arrangement room. "Time for introductions."

They circled up — Fa at her desk chair, Larry on the edge of a sofa, a couple of attendants leaning against the wall. Mulligan sat in the middle of the rug like he was about to hold court.

I said, "All right, buddy. Do your thing."

He cleared his throat — actually cleared it — and started.

Like many individuals, I have pursued several different careers throughout my professional life.
When I was a pup, I belonged to a man named *Jefe*. Nice wardrobe, terrible morals. He ran a small import-export operation, heavily weighted toward imports. My job was simple — sit in the room and tell him who was lying. Turns out that's an easy skill for a dog; people smell different when they fib.
Anyway, one day I told the truth to the wrong man and decided I'd better relocate myself."

The staff chuckled. Larry rolled his eyes. Fa leaned forward, grinning despite herself.

Mulligan went on.
"I hit the streets, learned a lot about dumpsters, and finally found refuge at the Presbyterian Night Shelter downtown. Nice folks. They had a women's and children's center that needed a night watchman with fur. I became the unofficial Service Dog in Residence — security on the outside, therapy on the inside.
I'd curl up beside the kids until they stopped shaking and let the mamas cry without feeling alone. Some nights, I'd sit outside the shower stalls so the little ones wouldn't be scared of the pipes banging.
Best work I ever did — until one of the staff decided I was too valuable to be free and sold me. Traded me for a used set of tires. Life lesson: never trust a man who drives on bald treads."

Fa snorted into her coffee.

Mulligan gave a slow, theatrical sigh. "Anyway, from there I bounced through a few homes — a police dog academy, a brief stint at a hospice where they said I had 'boundary issues' because I kept climbing in beds — and that's where I met Georgette, a champion standard poodle with legs like poetry. We volunteered at children's hospitals together — I told the jokes; she did the glamour.

The kids loved her. They said I looked like her *before* picture. That's when I realized ugly and beautiful can serve the same purpose — making people forget the hard stuff for a while."

He paused, scanned the room, and fixed his eyes on Larry.

"So, next time somebody — *Larry* — calls me ugly…" he said, voice dropping an octave, "…I will bite their ass."

Silence. Then the entire room broke open laughing.

Larry wiped tears. "Fair enough, partner. Fair enough."

That was all it took. Fa was down on her knees, scratching his ears. The attendants joined in, cooing like grandmas at a baby shower.

"Who's the good boy?"
"Such a smart boy!"

Mulligan blinked at me, deadpan. "In dog years, I'm older than most of you. Cut out the baby talk."

The laughter doubled.

I leaned against the doorway, just watching it happen — this strange, warm ripple of joy moving through a place that had carried too much quiet for too long.

When things finally settled, I patted his back. "All right, partner, let's hit the pet store. We've got supplies to buy."

He trotted down the aisle beside me like a professional shopper, his nose working overtime.

"All right," I said, "what do we need?"
He stopped at a display and started dictating.
"Four memory-foam beds — one for me, one for Anna Belle, and one for Teddy for the home, and one for the office. Stainless bowls. Chicken treats, none of that grain-free cardboard. And a proper brush; Fa said I'm 'adorably ugly,' but we can aim for *less ugly*."

I loaded the cart while he supervised, tail flicking like a metronome.
We were almost out the door when he froze in front of a display, the size of a small refrigerator.

On it sat the K-9 Ballistic Fetch Pro 3000.

The box promised *automatic, programmable, tournament-grade tennis-ball propulsion.*
I laughed. "You don't need that! I'll throw you a ball myself."
He shook his head. "It's not for me, Cole. It's for your staff. They all look like they need cardio."

I stared. He stared back.
"That's ridiculous," I said.
He grinned. "You say that like it's a bad thing."

So, we bought it.

Back at the funeral home, the crew watched us unload the contraption into the back parking lot.
Fa squinted. "What on earth is that?"
"Our new wellness program," I said.
Mulligan pressed the start button with his paw. The machine hummed, then fired a tennis ball across the lot like a mortar shell.

"Line up!" he barked. "Sheridan & Son Fitness Initiative, Session One!"

To my surprise, they did.
Larry lumbered after the first ball. Fa chased the second, pretending she wasn't enjoying herself. Someone filmed it from the chapel

window. Passing cars slowed.

For five glorious minutes, the world forgot it was a funeral home.

Finally, I called it off. Larry was red-faced and wheezing. Mulligan trotted over, tongue lolling, proud as a drill sergeant.

"Not bad, I give them three weeks before they're ready for nationals."

"Nationals?" I asked.

"Trust the program," he said.

We stood there watching the staff catch their breath, laughter echoing off the brick.

As the sun dipped behind the chapel roof, Mulligan looked up at me, his expression was softer now.

"Anna Belle and Teddy filled me in," he said quietly. "Why the house feels so sad. They love Julia and Dane. They're trying."

He sat beside me, eyes steady. "You've heard my story, Cole. Now you owe me yours. The whole one."

I nodded.

He wagged once. "Good. I like stories with heart."

Chapter 5 — The Whole Story

That evening, we sat on the back porch, the air thick with that Texas-evening stillness you can almost hear. The cicadas were tuning up, and the porch light had just started to hum. Mulligan lay beside my chair, chin on his paws, eyes bright and waiting.

"Well, Mulligan," I said, "you asked for my story. Guess I'll start with Julia."

He nodded. "Good place to start. Most miracles begin with somebody who can't be replaced."

"Julia was born and raised in Santa Anna," I began. "She spent kindergarten through high school there and still loves that little town. Her dad, Burl, grew up just north of there — poor as church dirt but smart as a whip.

"After high school, he started college. Then World War II began, and the Army sent him to England. Because he had some college, they stuck him behind a typewriter — 'administrative duties.' A rough-and-tumble Texas boy typing requisition forms. He hated it."

Mulligan's tail twitched. "Sounds like putting a cattle dog in charge of the stationery."

"Exactly. He volunteered for the infantry and ended up at the Battle of the Bulge. Survived that frozen hell, came home, finished college, and became an accountant. But that wasn't enough. He drilled an oil well with his cousin, hit pay dirt, and spent the rest of his life running a small oil-and-gas company and a ranch outside Santa Anna. He worked hard every day until the end."

Mulligan sighed softly. "Good men usually do. They mistake purpose for oxygen."

"He met Dane not long after he got back. She was from an even smaller town north of there, even poorer. They married young. She loved being a mother and the woman of the house.

"Then tragedy hit. Their little boy — Julia's baby brother — got sick at three. They brought him to Fort Worth for treatment, but he didn't make it. Seventy-plus years later, his picture's still by her bed."

Mulligan's ears lowered. "Dogs know about that kind of loyalty. We never bury love; we guard it quieter."

"She's done just that," I said. "After that loss, she poured herself into caring for Julia and Burl. Julia grew up smart, beautiful, and proud of her roots.

During her final year, she was named Texas Pecan Queen. She shared that although she was offered the title of Mixed Nuts Queen the following year, she declined to avoid being typecast.

Mulligan snorted. "Queen of pecan and praline — there are worse legacies."

"After graduation, she went to the University of Texas. Still bleeds burnt orange. When she left for Austin, Dane returned to college, earned her degree in education, and became a teacher.

"Julia graduated, moved to Fort Worth. She loved Santa Anna, but she had bigger dreams. Started in banking, worked her way up, and retired when Burl's health began slipping."

Mulligan looked impressed. "Ambitious and loyal — double-rare breed."

"That's about the time I met her," I said. "At the Colonial National Invitational golf tournament. I was divorced, not looking. But I found someone. The best find of my life."

He grinned. "Love never uses turn signals."

"When she took me to meet Burl and Dane, she warned me they might be surprised. She told me about her little brother who died at three — his name was Cole Clint.

"So, there I was — Cole — and my boy — Clint. She said sometimes she thinks God still writes His jokes in longhand."

Mulligan nodded. "He's got a distinctive sense of humor."

"Burl and Dane took us in like we'd been theirs all along. Burl and I bonded instantly — sports, politics, weather, whatever came up."

Mulligan wagged. "If friendship were a leash, that man had you collared."

"You could say that. I learned to keep gloves in my pocket. When Burl asked, 'Wanna go for a ride?' it meant mending fences or moving cattle — not sightseeing."

He chuckled. "You humans use 'ride' too loosely."

"Burl loved baseball — especially the Rangers. I was friends with Eddie Robinson, the old Yankee and Rangers GM, and we started the Major League Players Alumni Golf Tournament. I'd bring Burl every year. He'd meet legends, shake hands, grin like a kid at Christmas."

"Baseball, barbecue, and bragging rights," Mulligan said. "The Holy Trinity of Texas."

"Pretty much. And as much as I loved him, Julia loved him more. He was her champion.

"When he fell at the post office and hit his head… by the time we got to the hospital, he was gone. I watched something leave Julia that day — something she'll never fully get back."

Mulligan's voice softened. "Grief doesn't take the whole heart. It just steals the part that laughs first."

"Dane grieved too, but quietly. She didn't want Julia to see it. Or she'd been grieving since her boy died.

"After the funeral, Julia took her back to the ranch. But when she went to leave, Dane got in the car and said, 'I can't stay here by myself.' So, she came to live with us."

"She's been with us ever since. Reads her Bible every morning, underlines like she's afraid to miss a verse. Ninety -six now — sharp as ever.

She and Julia are very much alike. Strong. Loving. Stubborn with a doctorate."

Mulligan stretched, paws out, eyes on the horizon. "Now I see why the house feels like that, three hearts carrying too much memory and one man trying to patch the roof with laughter."

I smiled. "That's about right."

He lifted his head. "Cole, grief's a pack animal. It sticks close until you give it a new job.

"Julia misses being somebody's daughter. Dane misses being somebody's wife and mother. And you — well, miss being able to fix things with your hands.

"I can't bring Burl back. But I can bring back the sound he loved most."

"What sounds like that?" I asked.

"Julia laughing, and if I have to juggle tennis balls, fake a British accent, and chase Larry around the parking lot every day to do it, then that's the mission."

I laughed quietly. "That's a tall order, Mulligan."

He stood, tail wagging slowly and sure. "Boss, I'm a talking dog bought for twenty bucks. Miracles are my department."

He nudged my arm. "Now then… You said there were other dogs in this story — Anna Belle, Teddy, and the ones before. I like to know the ancestors. Let's hear about them next."

And just like that, the old porch filled with something we hadn't felt in a while.

Anticipation.

The kind that sounds a lot like hope clearing its throat.

Chapter 6 — Julia's Pack

"You know, Mulligan," I said, leaning back in my porch chair, "you're one very lucky little boy."

Lying across the porch rug, his eyes partly closed, he lifted his gaze. "Lucky? I was bought off a yard-sale sign for twenty dollars."

"Exactly," I said. "That's what makes it so impressive. You landed in the right place."

He gave a modest shrug. "Some call it luck. I call it divine intervention."

I laughed. "Well, around here, you've joined a long line of four-legged saints. Most of Julia's friends say that if there's reincarnation, they want to come back as one of Julia's pets."

Mulligan grinned. "Do they get room service and health insurance?"

"Pretty much. And home-cooked meals."

His ears perked. "You're not joking, are you?"

"Nope. Not even a little."

"Julia grew up on a ranch," I said, "so animals have always been part of her world — dogs, cows, even a horse she loved like kin. When that horse died, Burl built a little cemetery out there on the property.

"Proper iron fence. Real markers. A bench under a big pecan tree. It's not for people; it's for the pets — their family."

Mulligan's tail moved once. "Now that's holy ground. A place where even those who remained silent are still remembered."

"Exactly. That horse was the first one buried there. And it's still the prettiest spot on the ranch."

"When Julia went to the University of Texas, she adopted a basset hound named Borrus. He got her through college, and then through the move to Fort Worth.

"She said he was stubborn, loyal, and flatulent — all the traits of a long relationship."

Mulligan nodded solemnly. "Good man, that Borrus. A real foundational type."

"You don't know this, Mulligan, but Julia was married once before me. A good man. Kind. Honest.

"There was a gun accident at the ranch — a misfire —, and he didn't make it.

"It shattered her."

Mulligan didn't speak for a long moment. Then, softly, he said, "That kind of loss leaves a permanent shadow. You learn to garden around it."

"After that," I continued, "she adopted a collie named Amy. Beautiful blonde dog. Pure grace. Amy helped her heal, little by little.

"Julia's always believed dogs are companions in many ways — physical, emotional, spiritual. But she also believes no one should ever be alone, so she adopted a beagle named Maggie to keep Amy company.

"Maggie was every bit a beagle — opinionated, loud, always convinced she knew better."

Mulligan smirked. "You're describing my aunt."

"When Julia and I started dating," I said, "the biggest test wasn't meeting her friends or her boss. It was meeting Amy and Maggie.

"I knew if the dogs didn't approve, I was done for."

"How'd you, do it?" Mulligan asked.

"Bribery," I said. "Chicken jerky and sincerity."

"Ah," Mulligan said. "The ancient art of diplomacy."

"During those years, we drove down to the ranch often. Burl and Dane had their own pack — Sam, the mighty Labrador, and JB, their border collie.

"Sam was built like a linebacker and thought wrestling was a competitive sport. He's the only dog I've ever met who could pin me to the floor and grin about it."

Mulligan grinned. "That's my kind of guy."

"JB, on the other hand, was brilliant — one of Tommy Lucia's border collies that performed at rodeos. Smart. Agile. Could herd people better than a preacher herds guilt.

"If you weren't careful, he'd corner you in your own house just to prove he could."

"And Lucy?" Mulligan asked.

"Ah, Lucy," I said. "Somebody dropped her near the ranch. Little pup, sweet as syrup. Dane took her in and spoiled her rotten. She was her baby.

"One day, Lucy poked her nose into the wrong dark corner of the barn. Rattlesnake.

"Burl buried her under the pecan tree beside the horse."

Mulligan lowered his head. "She's got good company."

"Julia and Dane take care of their animals like royalty," I said. "Half the time, they cook for them — liver, chicken, rice, carrots. All homemade."

Mulligan shuddered. "Please tell me dessert isn't kale."

"No kale. But if you like liver, you're in luck."

"I was hoping for prime rib," he muttered.

"Over the years, we've lost some and saved some.

"There was another collie we rescued — already eaten up with heartworms — but we gave him a few good years.

A cocker spaniel that had suffered abuse. We did our best with him, too."

Mulligan nodded. "That is the thing about rescue work. You don't fix the world; you prove it's still worth trying."

"Then came Anna Belle. Julia thought she was getting a regular beagle, but she turned out to be a blue tick — stubborn, opinionated, and about half as obedient as she is cute.

"She runs the house."

"I've noticed," Mulligan said dryly. "She has management potential."

"And then Teddy. Julia wanted another blonde collie like Amy, but the universe sent us a black one who looks like he's still deciding what breed he wants to be.

"I found him in a trailer park that was worse on the inside than the outside. I nearly walked away, but he looked at me like he was out of options.

"So, I brought him home. He turned out to be one of the best decisions I've ever made."

"Good save," Mulligan said. "We mutts always test your faith before we reward it."

"For Dane, Julia found a standard poodle named George — mighty, black, proud, loyal. He was her constant companion for years.

"After he passed, I could tell she was quietly grieving. You'd be surprised, Mulligan — after fifty years in funeral service — how many kinds of grief you can recognize."

Mulligan looked up. "I've seen it too. People don't always cry; sometimes they stare at a doorway too long."

"One day I asked her, 'Dane, if you could have another dog, what would it be?'

"She said, 'I'd love another standard poodle like George.'"

Mulligan wagged. "That's how miracles start — with a sentence said to the right listener."

"When Burl passed, it hit Julia hard. She's tough — proud Texas tough — but losing him cracked something deep.

"And then, only a few days later, Charlie, her black cocker spaniel, died suddenly.

"That one-two punch nearly undid her."

I shook my head. "You'd think after fifty years in funeral service, I'd have the words. But I didn't.

"You spend a lifetime comforting others, and one day you realize you can't fix your own."

Mulligan sat up, ears forward, eyes steady. "Cole, that's why I'm here."

"Because I needed a talking dog?"

He smiled gently. "Because you needed someone who listens without thinking about what to say next.

"You've been everyone else's comfort for half a century. Now it's your turn.

"And I'll make sure Julia and Dane laugh again — even if I have to fake a limp and pretend to be French."

I chuckled. "Lord help me, I think you mean it."

"I do," he said. "Besides, I hear there's liver for dinner."

I laughed, and for a while we just sat there — man and mutt — quiet, listening to the night breathe.

After a moment, Mulligan lifted his head, studying me like he was lining up his next question.

"Okay, you've told me about Burl and Dane. You've told me about Julia, Anna Belle, Teddy, and half the canine population of Texas…"

He paused, his tail twitching.

"But you haven't told me anything about you."

He tilted his head, eyes gentle but sharp.

"What's your story, Cole?"

Chapter 7 — My Story

Chapter 7 — My Story

Well, Mulligan," I said, leaning back in my chair, "you want the long version or the Cliff Notes?"

He lifted one eyebrow. "Cliff Notes? Please. I've got time, kibble, and a nap scheduled for later. Give me the long one."

"Fair enough," I said. "Just don't bite my ass if it gets boring."

He grinned. "No promises."

"I actually wrote a book about my life once," I said. "But you're getting the unabridged version." I was born right here in Fort Worth into a very Catholic family. My dad ran the funeral home. He left before the sun was up and came home after it went down. He devoted his life to funeral service and to the families he served. So, I learned from the best."

Mulligan nodded. "Sounds like a man who understood purpose better than sleep."

"He did," I said. "My mom was a Yankee from Toledo, Ohio — also very Catholic. If it had anything to do with the Church, we would be in the front row. I went to Catholic schools from first grade through high school. We weren't poor, but we sure weren't rich either. Being one of six kids eats up any loose change."

Mulligan chuckled. "I've seen litters like that. Someone is always chewing on someone else's shoe."

"Exactly. I loved scouting — became an Eagle Scout — and I'm still proud of that to this day. Then came my senior year. It was January 1st, a little after nine at night, when my dad came to me and said, 'You've been wanting a job.' I've got one for you.'"

Mulligan wagged. "Let me guess — dog walking?"

"Nightman," I said. "At the funeral home."

He blinked. "That escalated quickly."

"Sure did. I said, 'Great." When do I start?' He said, 'Right now." Go relieve your grandmother.' That night, I began my funeral career. I kept that job through college, then went on to mortuary school to earn my license. Married Clint's mom, and life ran smoothly for a while."

"I've always loved golf," I said. "Started playing when I was ten. I still love it today. The course is where I unwind — even when I'm losing. Which is often."

"Golf's a strange sport," Mulligan said. "You hit a tiny ball into a faraway hole and then act surprised when it doesn't listen."

"That's about right," I said. "Anyway, Clint's mom and I eventually went our separate ways. Life does that sometimes. Then I met Julia at the Colonial. Best decision of my life."

"Our funeral home back then ran like clockwork. My dad was the best. My older brother — who I always tried to emulate — ran the business alongside him. We had a great staff, loyal families, and a solid reputation."

Then, in the mid-nineties, my brother got sick.

Before we knew it, he was gone.

Mulligan's ears lowered. "Losing a brother changes the whole rhythm of the house."

"It did," I said. "The vibe at the funeral home changed, and so did the family. By the late nineties, I was out. No job. No plan. They had me under a non-compete clause that said I couldn't work or own a funeral home anywhere near Fort Worth. So, I had to leave the town I loved. For a while, my family and I didn't speak."

"That's a special kind of grief," Mulligan said softly. "The kind where everyone's still breathing, but the silence feels like a cemetery."

"Exactly. I moved to a small community near here. I didn't know a soul, but I knew what my dad taught me — how to serve families. I built a new funeral home from the ground up. It took off. The community welcomed me. Business thrived. And for a while, it all felt right again."

"Then I made my worst decision," I said. "I took on a partner."

Mulligan winced. "Oh no. This sounds like one of those don't sign anything moments."

"You got it. At first, he seemed fine — smart, charming, and ambitious. Turned out he was about as trustworthy as that rattlesnake that took Lucy. After a few years, he drained the company's resources. In a blink, everything I'd built was gone."

Mulligan growled softly. "If you ever need me to pay him a visit, I'm licensed in Texas for motivational biting."

"I appreciate the offer," I said. "The only thing I got out of that deal was that I didn't sign a non-compete this time. I could work again — anywhere."

"So, I took over a small corporate funeral home in that same community. The deal was simple: I'd get a percentage of the gross profit. They thought they were hiring a placeholder. I turned that place around — from losing money every year to making more profit than some of their senior vice presidents."

Mulligan grinned. "You out-funeraled the corporation."

"I did," I said. "Which meant I was making more money than the people above me. And you know how that goes — the folks upstairs don't like it when the guy downstairs starts shining too bright."

He nodded. "Tall-poppy syndrome. Or in your world, tall-casket syndrome."

"Exactly. So, they cut me loose. Again."

"That's when Clint and I came back to Fort Worth. My dad had passed away years before. My non-compete was over. We decided to build something different—a funeral home that offered exceptional care and excellent value. We created it ourselves, investing everything into the project personally. It succeeded, attracting families and prompting a community response. It truly felt like home once more.

Mulligan wagged. "Full circle. That's how good stories end — or start over."

"Five years ago," I said, "my oldest sister — who I hadn't talked to much in years — called. The hospital wanted to buy our old family funeral home property. None of them wanted to keep the business. She asked if Clint and I wanted to buy it, with one catch — we'd have thirty days to move it."

Mulligan tilted his head. "Thirty days? That's not a move. That's a jailbreak."

"Exactly. But like all good Sheridan's, I said yes before I thought about it. And to make it interesting, that's when COVID hit."

He whistled. "You do like your uphill climbs."

"I found an old church that hadn't seen a remodel since before Reagan. Julia and I poured everything we had into that place — time, sweat, money, prayer. We turned it into a masterpiece. Beautiful chapel. Stained glass. Reception hall. Parking for miles. It's the finest funeral facility in the city — and I'll stand by that."

Mulligan nodded, serious now. "I've seen it. It's not just a building, Cole. It's a promise you kept."

"Thank you," I said quietly. "But it's not in the same zip code as our old families. And people are creatures of habit. Some of the old family names I see now in the paper — at other funeral homes — folks who were close to my dad, even close friends. And I wonder if I made a mistake. Maybe I've just run out of luck."

"I'm tired, Mulligan," I admitted. "Inside, I still feel like the guy who could do it all. But outside… sometimes I can't keep up. I love this work. I love this city. I love the people who trust us when their world falls apart. I just don't know if I've got another big rebuild left in me."

Mulligan didn't move for a long moment. Then he sat up, eyes steady, voice low.

"Cole, you know what I've learned from all your stories tonight?"

"What's that?"

"You never stayed down. Not once. You've been buried more times than your own caskets, and yet here you sit — still building, still serving, still loving people who've already forgotten how lucky they are to have you."

He stood, stretched, his tail wagging slowly and surely.

"Maybe you're not running out of luck. Maybe luck just finally showed up with four paws and a loudmouth."

I smiled. "So, you're the miracle, huh?"

He grinned. "Miracle? No. More like divine pest control. But I'll take credit if it helps."

We sat there for a while, the night wrapping around us, quiet except for the hum of the porch light and the sound of possibility settling in.

Sometimes miracles don't arrive in the nick of time.

Sometimes they walk in, smell faintly of bacon, and refuse to leave until you start believing again.

Chapter 8 — The Lady in White (and I Don't Mean a Ghost)

Chapter 8 — The Lady in White

(and I Don't Mean a Ghost)

Saturday morning, Julia convinced me to go with her and Dane to a charity event at the children's hospital. They were hosting a showcase of therapy and comfort animals — dogs, ponies, rabbits, even a goat in a tutu who looked as if he regretted all his life choices.

I parked out front, and the four of us walked inside. The lobby was full of wagging tails and smiles.

But the second we stepped through the doors, Mulligan froze.

His nose twitched. One ear went up. That coffee-colored stare locked onto something across the room.

Then, in a voice just above a whisper, he said, "No way."

Across the lobby, a handler in scrubs knelt beside a little boy in a wheelchair. Resting her chin on the boy's lap — white fur glowing under the hospital lights — was a standard poodle named Georgette.

The same name.

The same grace.

The same story Mulligan had told me the day I bought him for twenty bucks.

Julia gasped. "She's beautiful."

Mulligan puffed out his chest. "Told you she was real."

I blinked. "You're saying that's the Georgette?"

He nodded slowly, eyes shining. "The one and only. We worked together back in my FBI -CIA multi-agency days. She specialized in emotional intelligence and tail etiquette."

Dane chuckled. "You expect us to believe that?"

Mulligan turned toward her, perfectly serious. "Ma'am, I don't expect belief. I expect respect. And maybe a treat."

Julia was already misty-eyed, watching the poodle comfort that child.

"Cole," she whispered, "look at her. She's not just a dog. She's… peace on four paws."

Mulligan sighed. "She always had that gift. She could calm a storm just by breathing."

The little boy giggled, hugging Georgette's neck, and for a moment every ache in the room seemed to lift. Julia squeezed my arm. Even Dane smiled — the quiet smile of a woman who'd underlined half her Bible and still believed in miracles.

Mulligan cleared his throat.

"Boss, I hate to interrupt your spiritual awakening, but we're bringing her home."

"Bringing her home?"

"She belongs with us. "With Julia. With Dane. With the families at the funeral home. We're meant to work together again. Destiny. Redemption. The whole dog -eared chapter."

Julia laughed. "You really think she remembers you?"

Mulligan tilted his head. "You never forget your first leash partner."

I shook mine. "Mulligan, she's clearly happy here."

"Happy, yes, Complete? No. Look at her eyes, she's glancing this way. She knows I'm here."

Dane leaned into me. "Cole, I think he's right. She is looking this way."

"She's looking at the donut table, Dane."

"Still," she said softly, "maybe this is a sign."

Mulligan's tail wagged with new purpose. "Exactly. A divine appointment. You don't ignore those."

I exhaled, already sensing where this was going. "So, what's your plan?"

He grinned. "Simple. We adopt her. I'll manage her orientation, emotional onboarding, advanced nap scheduling — you know, the essentials. You sign the papers."

Julia looked up at me with that familiar spark — the one I hadn't seen since before Burl passed.

"Cole," she said, "maybe we should look into it."

Mulligan sat taller, proud as a preacher. "See? Even humans agree. Faith, family, and the pursuit of paw -sitivity."

Dane chuckled under her breath. "Lord help us all."

Mulligan's eyes softened. "He already has," he said. "Her name's Georgette."

Chapter 9 — Fetch, Fatso, Fetch

Chapter 9 — Fetch, Fatso, Fetch

The next morning, when we pulled into the parking lot, Larry was standing out in front with a tennis ball in one hand and a cup of coffee in the other.

His shirt was untucked, his tie hanging somewhere between half-staff and surrender.

Mulligan spotted him immediately. "Ah, a man ready for his morning workout."

Larry squinted. "Workout? I'm waiting on my kolache."

"Then consider this divine intervention," Mulligan replied, tail flicking.

Inside, the staff lit up when they saw us.

Fa grinned. "We were afraid you weren't bringing him today."

"Don't worry," I said. "At this rate, he's going to be Employee of the Month."

"Again," Mulligan added.

Fa knelt to pet him. "You're adorable, but you still need a bath."

Larry took a sip of coffee. "Adorable? That dog looks like he fell out of a moving pickup."

Mulligan turned, slow and deliberate. "Next time you call me ugly, Fatso, I'll bite your ass."

The room went silent for half a beat — then erupted in laughter.

Fa nearly spilled her coffee. Larry turned red but smiled, shaking his head. "You talk a big game, mutt."

"Better than playing a small one," Mulligan shot back.

I cleared my throat. "All right, folks — let's stick to the funeral schedule before HR gets involved."

After the meeting, I brought Mulligan back to my office.

He jumped into my chair like he owned the place.

"Cole I've been thinking about our next move."

"That's never good," I muttered.

"Hear me out," he said, ignoring me. "We bring Georgette onboard as our new comfort dog. Think about it — Cole Sheridan & Son Funeral Home, home to the most compassionate, best-groomed, dual-certified grief-support team in Texas. I'll handle her training personally."

"Training?" I raised an eyebrow. "Mulligan, you've never trained anyone in your life."

He leaned back, smug as a senator at a ribbon-cutting. "Wrong. I told you when we met — I speak both Dog and Human. That makes me twice as qualified as anyone else. Besides, Georgette already knows the basics. I'll add some flair."

"Flair?"

"Funeral flair. Graceful entrances. Calming presence. Proper hymn etiquette. She'll be perfect."

"Perfect for what?" I asked.

"For saving your business and Julia's spirit," he said matter-of-factly. "Face it, boss — we've been running low on miracles. Time to restock."

Before I could reply, Larry poked his head in. "Hey, Boss — you gotta see this."

Out in the parking lot, the staff had gathered. The K-9 Ballistic Fetch Pro 3000 launcher was set up like an artillery piece.

"Team-building exercise," Mulligan announced. "We're boosting morale and cardio. Everyone gets three throws and one emergency defibrillator."

Fa laughed so hard she had to lean on the hearse.

Larry rolled up his sleeves and stepped to the line like a man heading into battle.

"Larry," Mulligan barked, "remember — bend your knees, chase with purpose, and if you collapse, collapse toward the ball."

He fired the launcher. The ball shot thirty yards. Larry puffed, wheezed, and returned with it like a retriever who regretted all his life choices.

"Good hustle, Fatso!" Mulligan yelled. "You're improving."

I finally shut it down when Larry looked about one throw away from seeing the light.

"Enough," I said. "Before we have to embalm one of our own."

Mulligan trotted over, tongue lolling, satisfied. "See, boss? Physical fitness, morale boost, and comic relief — all in one exercise. We're unstoppable."

Back in my office, I sat down and looked at him.

"Mulligan, I don't know how you do it, but somehow you've got everyone smiling again."

He shrugged. "That's what I do. And once we bring Georgette into the fold, we'll double the joy. She's elegance, I'm charm. Together, we're healing with fur."

I smiled. "You really think she'll come with us?"

He looked out the window, quiet for once. "I think she's been waiting for me to come back."

Then he turned to me, eyes soft. "Anna Belle and Teddy told me why the house feels heavy. They love Julia and Dane, but it's quiet — too quiet. Georgette could change that. She can bring light back where the dark's been sitting too long."

He hopped down and stretched. "So, you get the paperwork, and I'll handle the pitch. Trust me, boss — I've still got a little magic left."

That night, as I locked up and headed for home, I caught Mulligan staring out the window toward the stars.

"Thinking about her?" I asked.

He didn't look away. "Just thinking how sometimes the lies we tell are really just hopes waiting for proof."

I smiled. "You really think you'll find your proof?"

He turned, that old grin returning. "I already have. She's got curls, class, and a heart big enough for all of us."

Chapter 10 — The Adoption

In the morning, we were supposed to go to the children's hospital, but Mulligan refused to get in the truck. He sat by the door, head high, tail twitching, like he was waiting on a limo instead.

"Let's go," I said, jingling the keys.

He didn't move. "Not like this."

"Not like what?"

He sighed dramatically. "Unkempt. Fa's right. I need a bath."

Julia looked up from her coffee. "You hate baths."

"I hate bad impressions more, squinting at his reflection in the window. "She deserves to see me at my best."

"Who's she?" I asked, even though I already knew.

He turned slowly, the way only someone in love—or full of themselves—can. "Georgette."

Ten minutes later, we pulled into the groomers. Julia was already laughing before I even parked. Mulligan strutted through the door like a celebrity checking in under an alias, hopped up with his front paws on the counter, and said, "I'd like to look like this."

He tapped the phone screen with his paw—an image of a Grand Champion Standard Poodle, every curl perfect, every hair pre-approved by the Lord Himself.

The groomer squinted. "Sweetheart, this is a poodle. You're… not."

Mulligan nodded solemnly. "Not on the outside. That's how I am inside. She'll see it."

Julia had to walk away to keep from laughing aloud. I just sighed and handed over my credit card.

Forty-five minutes later, the groomer emerged covered in fur and looked like she'd wrestled a sheep during allergy season.

"Finished," she said weakly.

Mulligan strutted out behind her, smelling like lavender and ego, his fur fluffed into something halfway between a dandelion and a perm gone rogue. He turned in a slow circle.

"Perfect, now I'm ready."

I looked him over. "You look like you lost a fight with a blow dryer."

"Art takes courage," he replied, hopping into the truck. "Let's roll. Destiny doesn't wait for dog breath."

When we arrived at the children's hospital, Julia and Dane were already waiting by the entrance. Mulligan leapt out, chest puffed, tail swishing in slow motion like he was in a shampoo commercial.

Inside, the crowd parted almost at once, as if he were the guest of honor. Someone whispered, "That's him—the talking dog from the event!"

Mulligan grinned. "Don't ruin my brand, boss."

Across the lobby, the volunteer coordinator smiled when she saw us. Beside her, just like before, sat Georgette, radiant as ever, her white coat glowing under the fluorescent lights.

The second she spotted us, her head tilted. She stood, took two delicate steps forward, and wagged her tail once, like a queen granting an audience.

"Georgette," Mulligan whispered, his voice trembling just enough to give him away.

Julia leaned down. "You think she remembers you?"

"She never forgot me," he said softly.

They met halfway across the room. Mulligan bowed—actually bowed—and Georgette leaned in, pressing her nose to his. For a long moment, no one spoke. Even the kids in the waiting area went quiet.

Then Mulligan said, "You look like you've been bathed in heaven and brushed by angels."

Georgette gave one dignified bark that somehow sounded like laughter.

The coordinator smiled. "Funny thing—her previous owner passed away last month. She's been staying here, but we've been looking for a new placement. She needs a real home."

Julia gasped. "Oh, Cole…"

Mulligan turned to me, tail flicking like a metronome. "See? Divine appointment. I told you."

I looked at Julia. She nodded before I even asked.

While Julia handled the adoption papers, Mulligan insisted on filling out his own version. He borrowed Dane's pen from her purse and scrawled something on a napkin.

"Clause one, Unlimited snacks. Clause two, shared couch privileges. Clause three, no kale."

The coordinator laughed. "Do you have other pets at home?"

Mulligan answered before I could. "Two canines, one theologian in training, and a retired ranch matriarch. All friendly. Mostly housebroken."

I handed her the check and prayed she didn't ask for references.

On the ride home, Georgette sat perfectly upright like royalty, while Mulligan sprawled across the seat like he was back in a college dorm.

"Sit up straight," I said. "You're setting a bad example."

"I'm showing her I'm comfortable being myself. It's called confidence."

Julia glanced over. "Mulligan, she's a lady."

"And I am a gentleman in training."

He sniffed toward Julia's Dr Pepper. "Speaking of ladies—may I?"

She sighed, handed him the can, and he took a polite lap. "Still the drink of miracles."

Anna Belle spotted them first through the window, barking twice, territorial but curious. Teddy followed, tail wagging cautiously.

When we opened the door, Mulligan trotted in first, chest out. "Everyone, this is Georgette. Try to act civilized."

Anna Belle growled once, then froze as Georgette bowed her head in greeting—graceful, unthreatening. The tension melted.

Teddy circled once, dropped a toy at Georgette's feet, and wagged. Instant friendship.

Mulligan nodded proudly. "See? Leadership potential. She's already promoted Teddy to Junior Fetch Manager."

Julia clapped her hands. "Look at them! They fit right in."

Dane smiled. "She's beautiful. Reminds me of my George."

Mulligan beamed. "You hear that, Georgie? You're making miracles already."

That night, Julia put on a movie, popcorn in the microwave, sodas on the counter, and everyone in their usual spots. Anna Belle trotted in proudly carrying the unopened bag of popcorn again, tail wagging as she'd just invented it.

Julia laughed. "Anna Belle, honey, you've got to let us open it first."

Mulligan muttered, "Every time. She's gonna die of unpopped potential."

Teddy curled up beside Georgette, who rested her head on Julia's lap. Dane read her Bible quietly from her chair. I leaned back, watching the glow of the TV wash over all of them—our odd little family of people and pups.

Mulligan glanced up at me, his voice low. "You know, boss, they think they adopted her. But we just adopted them."

I smiled. "Maybe twenty dollars doesn't buy much these days," I said. "But it's sure bought us a lot of miracles."

Mulligan grinned, eyes half-closed. "And this one comes with conditioner."

Chapter 11 — The Comfort Dog Team

The next morning, the house was humming. Julia was humming. Dane was humming. Even the coffee pot was humming—mostly because Mulligan had tried to pour himself a cup.

"Big day," he said, tail wagging as he straightened the little red bow tie Julia had fastened around his neck. "Public debut of the Sheridan Comfort Dog Team. Dignity, decorum, and maybe a light lunch."

"Lunch?" I asked.

"Emotional work burns calories, boss, dead serious. "You'll learn."

Georgette stood beside him, pristine and composed, like the vice president of good manners. Anna Belle and Teddy watched from the couch—Anna Belle was jealous, Teddy was curious.

"Don't worry," Mulligan told them. "You'll get your turn. Right now, it's strictly the A-Team."

When we pulled up at Guy Sheridan Funeral Home, Fa and Larry were already outside. Fa's smile widened the second she saw the two dogs step out of the truck.

"Oh, Mulligan, you finally got your bath!"

He nodded proudly. "Yes, ma'am. It's amazing what a little soap and self-esteem can do."

Larry grinned. "Well, look at you. And who's this fancy lady?"

"This," Mulligan said, puffing out his chest, "is Georgette. My professional partner, emotional support specialist, and co-founder of our outreach division.

Georgette gave one elegant bark.

Fa knelt to pet her. "Oh, she's gorgeous."

"She's more than that," Mulligan said. "She's grace with fur. You're lucky to have us both."

"Us?" I said.

He ignored me. "Now, before we begin, I'd like to say a few words."

I sighed. "Here we go."

The staff gathered near the front counter. Mulligan cleared his throat theatrically, like a preacher warming up.

"I suppose most of you have heard the rumors," he began. "Yes, it's true. I was once owned by a man named Jefe—not a pleasant fellow. But that's not the story I want to tell today."

Fa giggled already.

"You see, long before I joined Cole Sheridan & Son, Georgette and I were partners—top-tier emotional first responders for the FBI's Division of Feelings."

"Division of Feelings?" Fa asked.

"That's right," Mulligan said solemnly. "Our mission: to bring comfort in crisis and wag tails where hope was fading. Hospitals, airports, and even a rodeo. She managed the fancy work; I managed logistics. "It was a wonderful collaboration up until she was transferred to children's hospitals, and I…" He hesitated. "Well, I took a sabbatical."

"Translation," I muttered, "he ran off and found bacon."

Mulligan ignored me. "But destiny, dear friends, has a way of reuniting those who belong together. And now, together again, we're here to serve."

Larry clapped slowly. "That's the best lie I've heard all week."

Mulligan wagged. "You'll learn, Fatso. The truth's just a lie that grew up."

After the event concluded, we gathered our belongings and proceeded to Cole Sheridan & Son Funeral Home, where my son Clint and his team were ready to receive us.

They'd heard about Mulligan, of course. Who hadn't? But seeing him in person, bow tie and all, was another matter.

Clint came out front, arms crossed but smiling. "Dad, I've heard about your new hire. He'd better not steal our clients."

Mulligan stepped forward. "Sir, I assure you—I only steal hearts."

Georgette glided in beside him, radiant as ever.

"Ladies and gentlemen," I said, "meet the Sheridan Comfort Dog Team—Mulligan and Georgette."

Polite applause followed. Then Mulligan raised his paw for silence.

"Since we're new acquaintances a brief history is in order."

I mouthed Oh no to Clint. He just grinned.

Mulligan began pacing like a TED Talker in fur. "As I mentioned earlier, I began my professional career under Jefe—a man whose ethics were… flexible. After escaping that toxic environment, I joined the Bureau—briefly. My true calling came when Georgette and I were selected for an elite international initiative: the United Nations Comfort Corps."

Georgette gave a delicate bark, right on cue.

"We traveled the world—hospitals in Paris, orphanages in Peru, once even a royal palace in England. Her job was to calm the room. Mine was to manage crowd control and biscuit security."

A tall guy named Wade scratched his head. "You're saying you worked for the United Nations?"

Mulligan nodded. "Unofficially. Freelance. Our credentials were revoked after the sausage buffet incident in Geneva."

Georgette sighed, shaking her head like she'd heard it all before.

Fa whispered to Clint, "he's full of it."

Clint smiled. "Yeah—but he tells it Well."

Mulligan finished with a bow. "And that, my friends, is why we're here—to serve families with grace, compassion, and the occasional tennis ball."

The room broke into laughter and applause. Even Clint clapped.

"Well," he said, "if you can get families laughing that easily, you're hired."

Mulligan shot me a smug look. "Told you. Marketing genius."

On the drive home, Mulligan leaned back against the seat, satisfied.

"Well, boss, I'd say that went beautifully."

I nodded. "You realize nobody believed a word of it, right?"

He smiled. "Maybe. But they wanted to. That's what matters."

Georgette gazed out the window, serene as a saint.

"Besides," Mulligan added softly, "some of it was true."

"Which part?" I asked.

He winked. "Wouldn't you like to know?"

Chapter 12 — The Family from Monterrey

It was one of those gray Texas mornings where the light never quite makes up its mind. I'd just finished a service when my phone rang.

"Cole Sheridan," I said.

The voice on the other end was gentle and steady—one I knew well. It was Maria, a hospice chaplain I'd worked with for years.

"Cole," she said softly, "I have a family I'd like to refer you to. They just lost their mother. They're new to Fort Worth, and I think they could use someone like you."

Someone like me. I wasn't sure what that meant anymore, but I thanked her and told her to send them over.

After I hung up, it hit me that my Spanish-speaking director, Rafael, was home with the flu. I looked at my phone, then down at Mulligan, who was stretched out under my desk like a shag carpet with opinions.

"Mulligan," I said, "I've got a problem. I have a family from Monterrey. I don't speak Spanish, and Rafael's out."

Mulligan opened one eye. "I speak perfect Spanish."

I froze. "You what?"

"Fluent, stretching. "Learned it from Jefe."

I stared at him. "So, Jefe's real?"

"Parts of him," Mulligan said with a smirk. "But the Spanish part's real. Want me to prove it?"

Before I could answer, he grabbed my phone with his paw, tapped the screen, and opened the translator app.

"Look," he said. "You type in English; it shows what I'm saying in Spanish. And since I can hear both, you'll be fine."

I blinked. "This is insane."

"Welcome to working with me."

By the time the family arrived, the lobby air was thick with both grief and gratitude. A man and his wife, their two grown children, and three grandchildren stepped through the door—the kind of family that holds hands without even realizing it.

Their mother, I learned later, had battled Alzheimer's for a decade.

"She was our light," the son said. "Even when she forgot our names, she never forgot love."

As they sat, Mulligan trotted forward, tail wagging slowly and respectfully. Georgette followed, poised and elegant, her calm like a living benediction.

I opened the translator app, but Mulligan shook his head.

"I've got this," he whispered.

Then he sat in front of the family and began—fluent, precise, perfect Spanish, warm as a hand on the shoulder.

"Buenas tardes," he said. "Mi nombre es Mulligan. Soy el perro que habla."

The grandchildren gasped, then giggled. Their father blinked twice before smiling in disbelief.

Mulligan went on, weaving the parts of his story that mattered—being rescued from a cruel man, learning to listen, discovering that sometimes words don't heal, but presence does.

Then his voice softened.

"Su madre no se ha ido del todo" "El amor no se pierde cuando la memoria se va. Solo cambia de lugar. Vive aquí."

He placed a paw on his chest.

The nine-year-old granddaughter reached out and touched his head.

"Te extraño, abuela," she whispered.

Georgette leaned gently against her side, letting the girl's tears soak into her white coat. The room fell quiet except for the hum of the air conditioning and an occasional sniffle.

I'd spent my life in funeral homes. I'd seen anger, disbelief, and numbness. But this felt different.

It felt holy.

When the tears eased, Mulligan looked back at me. "You can take it from here, boss."

I swallowed hard and nodded.

With his help, we set the service details. The family wanted something simple—a Mass in Spanish, soft guitar music, her rosary displayed alongside photographs from Monterrey.

"She loved yellow," the daughter said. "It reminded her of sunshine and mangoes."

"Yellow it is," I said.

After the family left, Mulligan and Georgette lay side by side in the reception room.

"You were great," I said quietly.

Mulligan looked up, tired but proud. "Jefe may have taught me the words," he said, "but that lady taught me the meaning."

Georgette rested her head on her paws, eyes half-closed, the faint scent of lavender lingering where the little girl had hugged her.

"Boss," Mulligan said after a long silence, "when people forget everything—their name, their home, their own reflection—love still remembers them. That's the part I understand."

I reached down and rubbed his ear. "You and me both, partner."

I watched through the window as the family loaded into their car. The grandchildren waved, and Mulligan lifted one paw in return.

"Tomorrow," I said, "we'll go see Father Ben. They'll need a priest who speaks Spanish."

Mulligan nodded. "And maybe a choir."

Georgette wagged her tail once.

They walked down the hall together—side by side, tails swaying in rhythm, a mismatched pair of grace and grit.

It hit me then.

They weren't just comfort dogs anymore.

They were something bigger.

Something sent.

Chapter 13 — Father Ben and the Choir

The following morning began as our good days usually did: Mulligan demanded two servings of bacon, while Georgette perfected her posture before the foyer mirror.

"We're going to see my brother," I told them, clipping on their leashes. "He's Father Ben. A real priest. So, try to behave."

Mulligan tilted his head. "Define behave."

"Don't say anything sacrilegious."

He wagged his tail. "Relax, boss. I've been blessed by more clergy than a bottle of holy water."

On the drive over, I caught myself smiling, thinking about Ben.

He's two years older than me. We shared a bedroom until high school, and I idolized him. He always did everything just a little better: better grades, better swing, better at staying out of trouble.

When he joined the Boy Scouts, I joined too. We both made Eagle. When he ran track, I ran track. I briefly considered the seminary, but my girlfriend pointed out I'd have to stop dating. That settled that.

Ben went on to Rome, studied at the Pontifical Gregorian University right in the Vatican, and then earned a Canon Law degree from Catholic University. These days, he's a parish priest with a dry wit and a loyal congregation who'd follow him anywhere.

He's one of the best men I know. Always has been.

And despite our different paths—him saving souls and me, well… helping them on the way—we're still two sides of the same calling.

Father Ben's parish sat on a tree-lined street, the pecans tall and wise as old parishioners. Inside, the church carried that familiar, comforting scent of polished wood and candles.

As we stepped through the doors, music drifted down the nave—the choir mid-rehearsal, harmonies rolling through the sanctuary like a gentle tide.

And then, of course, Mulligan froze.

He glanced at Georgette. She gave him a look.

Before I could whisper, " Don't even think about it, they both lifted their heads and joined in.

It wasn't barking. It was music.

Mulligan's voice was low and soulful. Georgette's soared, light, and pure. Together they created something absurdly beautiful, the kind of harmony that makes you believe angels might lean in to listen.

The choir stopped.

The organist stopped.

The last note echoed through the rafters like a final Amen.

Then came a familiar voice from the back of the church.

"Cole," Ben called out, "please tell me you're finally joining the choir."

There he was—my big brother—same steady stride, same calm grin that used to drive me crazy when I'd lose an argument.

"Ben," I said, shaking his hand. "You've met stranger parishioners, I'm sure."

"Not ones that shed," he said, glancing at Mulligan. "And who are these angels with fur?"

Mulligan stepped forward, chest out. "Father, I'm Mulligan. This is Georgette. We're comfort professionals. Also, part-time vocalists. Non-denominational, of course."

Ben laughed. "I should've known my brother's ministry would eventually include talking dogs."

"I prefer to think of it as outreach," I said.

Ben folded his arms and looked down at Mulligan. "So, what's your story?"

Mulligan inhaled deeply, like a priest beginning a homily.

"Well, Father, I started my career working for an unsavory man named Jefe—translation, not confession. After seeing the error of my ways, I dedicated myself to spiritual work. I spent time at a Carmelite monastery helping the sisters bake communion wafers."

Ben smiled politely. "That's quite the ministry."

"It was," Mulligan said, "until I accidentally ate the inventory. Honest mistake. They looked like crackers."

Georgette nodded solemnly.

"After that," Mulligan continued, "we accepted a position at a synagogue. Wonderful people. Strong community. Unfortunately, I chased the rabbi's cat during Friday prayers. Another dismissal. We're currently between denominations."

Ben was laughing so hard he had to remove his glasses.

"Mulligan," catching his breath, "you may be the most ecumenical creature I've ever met."

"I try," Mulligan said proudly. "Inclusion matters."

When the laughter faded, I told Ben about the family from Monterrey—their loss, Mulligan's Spanish, and their need for a priest who could lead the Mass.

Ben's humor softened into something more profound. "Of course,." "We'll do it here. I'll say the Mass myself. Tell the family they are in good hands."

Then he looked back at the dogs. "And you two—I expect to see you back for choir practice."

Mulligan's tail wagged. "Do we get vestments?"

"No," Ben said, smiling, "but I'll make sure there are dog biscuits afterward."

As we headed out, the choir resumed. Mulligan glanced at Georgette, let out a soft woo, and soon they were harmonizing again.

Ben shook his head and leaned toward me. "You know, Cole—Dad used to say laughter was God's second language."

I smiled. "Yeah. These two might be fluent."

Standing there with my brother, two improbable comfort dogs, and the echo of their unlikely hymn filling the church, I realized how right Dad had been.

Because sometimes grace doesn't whisper.

Sometimes it howls—

perfectly in tune.

Chapter 14 — The Funeral Mass

The following morning started with what Mulligan called spiritual rehearsal. I called it chaos.

Julia had set out breakfast—scrambled eggs, toast, and a side of mild panic. Georgette sat at the table, posture regal, while Mulligan paced the kitchen floor, humming scales like a tenor warming up for Carnegie Hall.

"You two ready for choir practice?" I asked.

Georgette nodded once. Mulligan lifted his nose into the air. "Always. But do you think Father Ben prefers Gregorian chant or a more contemporary tail -wagging beat?"

"Just try not to upstage the sopranos."

"No promises," he said.

The choir loft at St. Timothy's smelled faintly of hymnals, perfume, and dust—the holy trinity of any Catholic church.

Father Ben was already there, laughing with the choir director, when we arrived. The organist glanced up, then down, then up again, unsure whether he was hallucinating or needed stronger glasses.

"Morning, Father," I said. "We're here to sign up your new members."

Ben smiled. "Excellent. I saved them a spot—right in the middle. Between the altos and the slightly tone -deaf retirees."

Mulligan hopped onto a chair and peered at the sheet music. "Ah. Ave Maria. Classic. You can't go wrong with Latin and pathos."

"Can you read music?" the choir director asked.

Mulligan winked. "I can read the room."

They began the opening bars, the organ filling the rafters with a soft, steady roll. Mulligan and Georgette tilted their heads, caught the pitch, and joined in—perfect, improbable harmony.

The altos gasped. The tenors grinned. Father Ben crossed his arms and whispered, "I've seen miracles before, but this is a first."

When the final note faded, the choir broke into applause. One older woman wiped her eyes. "I felt that right in my rosary."

Ben looked at me. "Cole, I think they're ready."

Mulligan puffed out his chest. "We'll need matching robes. Preferably satin."

That Monday, the church was full.

The Monterrey family filled the front pews, their faces a quiet blend of sorrow and peace. The altar was draped in white linen, and Father Ben's voice carried steady and warm through the sanctuary.

The Mass was entirely in Spanish—gentle, melodic, every prayer rising like incense.

Mulligan sat near the side aisle, wearing a tiny choir stole that Georgette had insisted upon. She stood beside him, still as marble, eyes soft and knowing.

When the choir sang, the two of them joined in, their harmony slipping seamlessly beneath the human voices. Heads turned, but no one seemed startled. If anything, the sound lifted the music higher, something that felt like it belonged there.

During the homily, Father Ben spoke not just of grief, but of presence.

"Even when memory fades, love remains. It never forgets the sound of your laughter or the rhythm of your prayers."

The family nodded through tears. The youngest granddaughter whispered, "Está aquí."

She's here.

The procession moved to the cemetery beneath a warm afternoon sun. Brass handles caught the light. The air smelled of fresh-cut grass and marigolds.

At the graveside, a small mariachi band waited—four men in black suits, silver embroidery gleaming, guitars and trumpets ready.

When the final prayer ended, they began Amor Eterno—slow, rich, heartbroken, and hopeful all at once.

Georgette pressed close to the family. Mulligan lay beside the casket, chin on his paws, tail moving faintly with the music.

When the song ended, Father Ben raised his hand. "May the angels lead her into paradise."

As if on cue, Mulligan lifted his head and howled once—low, steady, reverent. Not mournful. More like an Amen the wind could carry.

Back at Guy Sheridan Funeral Home, the reception hall glowed with soft light and the smell of tamales and sweet bread. Maria had arranged everything—yellow flowers, candles, framed photos of the matriarch smiling in younger days.

Georgette stationed herself with the children, accepting bits of tortilla with quiet dignity. Mulligan moved among the guests, offering what he called "grief counseling with snacks."

When the mariachi group joined us for one last song, laughter slipped between the verses, the kind that comes when tears finally loosen their grip.

Father Ben stood beside me, coffee in hand. "This is how it's supposed to be, Grief and joy holding hands."

"Yeah," I said. "It's a good day for a goodbye."

Across the room, Mulligan raised a glass of water, which he insisted was holy. "To Señora Morales, may heaven be filled with mariachi music and unlimited dog biscuits."

Ben laughed. "You realize Dad's shaking his head somewhere."

"Probably," I said. "But he's smiling too."

As the guests drifted out, the youngest granddaughter hugged Mulligan one last time. "Gracias, perrito," she whispered.

He licked her hand gently. "De nada, pequeña."

When the room finally emptied, the last notes of music still seemed to hang in the air. Light poured through the chapel windows, turning everything gold.

And I could almost hear Dad's voice slowly and certain.

You did right today, son.

Mulligan looked up at me. "You hear that too, don't you?"

I nodded. "Yeah, boy. I do."

Chapter 15 — Movie Night Revival

It started the way most good family stories do — with a dog and a bad idea.

Dinner was done, dishes stacked, and the house finally quiet. Julia was reading, Dane sat at the kitchen table with a Dr Pepper, and I was half-dozing in my chair, one shoe on, one shoe off — the picture of productivity.

Then came the sound of plastic crinkling across the floor.

Anna Belle trotted into the living room carrying an unopened bag of popcorn — unopened, mind you — and dropped it squarely in front of me like an offering.

Julia looked up from her book. "Well," she said, "someone's ready for movie night."

Mulligan, who'd been sprawled out on the rug, lifted his head, one ear cocked. "Movie night?" he asked. "Finally. I thought this family had gone fully documentary."

Teddy came bounding in right behind Anna Belle, tail wagging so hard he was practically sweeping the floor. Georgette followed last, deliberate, and graceful, settling beside Dane's chair like she owned the room.

Dane chuckled softly. "Well, looks like the gang's all here."

Mulligan sat up, straight-backed and serious. "If we're doing this, we're doing it right. I've taken the liberty of compiling a list."

Julia raised an eyebrow. "A list?"

He nodded. "The definitive Top Ten Dog Movies of All Time, ranked by artistic merit, cultural impact, and number of snacks consumed while watching."

Mulligan's Top Ten Dog Movies

He cleared his throat, as if announcing a eulogy.

Old Yeller — "The classic. Equal parts loyalty and trauma."

Homeward Bound — "An underrated road movie with excellent moral structure."

Beethoven — "A slobber-based masterpiece."

Benji — "Low budget, high heart."

Turner & Hooch — "Copaganda, but forgivable for the chemistry."

Because of Winn-Dixie — "Simple, sincere, and full of carbs."

The Art of Racing in the Rain — "Emotionally manipulative. Ten out of ten. Would watch again."

A Dog's Purpose — "My spiritual autobiography, if you skip the reincarnation bits."

Lady and the Tramp — "Reserved for special occasions."

The Secret Life of Pets — "Pure fiction. No one talks that much."

Julia laughed so hard she had to wipe her eyes. "So, what's the pick?"

Mulligan looked toward the others. Anna Belle was sitting tall, tail wagging. Teddy tilted his head, as if trying to understand the nominations. Georgette stared at the TV remote, as though she might control it telepathically.

"Tonight," Mulligan said, "we watch Lady and the Tramp."

Julia smiled. "That's not even in your top five."

He shrugged. "It's not about rankings. It's about romance. Tradition. And spaghetti."

Popcorn, Dr Pepper, and a Little Light

We popped the popcorn — two bags, because Teddy kept stealing handfuls when no one was looking. Dane insisted on pouring it into her old blue Tupperware bowl, the one with the crack down the side.

"This one holds the memories better," she said.

When the movie started, the room glowed with that soft, golden light that comes from an old TV and a happy story. Julia curled up beside me on the couch. Dane sat in her favorite chair, a blanket over her knees. Georgette climbed up next to her and lay her head gently on Dane's leg.

Dane stroked her ears, smiling. "You remind me of my George," she said quietly. "Same sweet eyes."

Georgette wagged once slowly and softly — then closed her eyes and stayed right there.

On the floor, Anna Belle stretched out in front of the screen, tail flicking every time the dogs on TV barked. Teddy positioned himself halfway between the popcorn bowl and Mulligan, ready for either opportunity.

When the spaghetti scene came on, Mulligan sighed contentedly. "Now this is cinema."

Julia leaned over. "You like this one, huh?"

He nodded. "It's a love story. Two dogs from different worlds, sharing one plate, one moment, one noodle." He paused dramatically. "That's the good stuff."

Dane giggled — really giggled — and for a moment, the whole house felt lighter.

After the Credits

When the movie ended, the room stayed quiet — the kind of silence you don't want to break.

Dane rubbed Georgette's head. "She even sighs the same way George did," she whispered.

Julia turned to me. "You know, we haven't had a night like this in a long time."

Mulligan stretched, yawned, and said, "Sometimes healing doesn't come in big moments. It sneaks in during the previews."

He settled back onto the rug, eyes half-closed, tail giving one last thump before drifting off.

As I looked around — Julia smiling softly beside me, Dane still petting Georgette, Anna Belle snoring, Teddy drooling, and Mulligan asleep at the center of it all — I realized the house didn't just look full again.

It felt full.

And for the first time in a long time, the silence was the good kind.

Chapter 16 — Family Night

By the time the sun slipped low, and the cicadas struck up their evening orchestra, the backyard was ready. The grill was hot, the Dr Peppers were chilling in the ice bucket, and the K-9 Ballistic Fetch Pro 3000 sat in the grass like a NASA prototype waiting for clearance.

Julia had made potato salad the way her mama taught her — heavy on the mustard, light on the logic — and Fa had wandered out with her glass of sweet tea muttering, "If that dog launches one of those balls through Julia's azaleas, she'll be the one doing the burial."

Mulligan was supervising from the patio, tail swinging like a metronome. Georgette, freshly groomed, looked radiant beside Dane, who sat under the patio fan with a light blanket over her knees and a smile that hadn't visited her face in months. Teddy and Anna Belle were stationed like sentries near the food table, ready to intercept anything edible that hit the ground.

Tonight was family night — and the first time Clint and the kids had properly met Mulligan and Georgette.

"Now, Mulligan," I said, turning burgers, "tonight you're going to meet my pride and joy — my son Clint and my grandkids Arnold and Amelia. You met Clint briefly at the funeral home, but tonight is the real deal."

Mulligan cocked an eyebrow. "Do I need a résumé?"

"Just good manners," I said. "Clint's the best funeral director I've ever known — maybe better than me."

Mulligan stopped wagging.

"Let me tell you something about him," I said, flipping a burger and watching the flames lick up. "So that you understand who you're dealing with."

He sat.

Not long ago, we lost a firefighter in a sudden, tragic incident that stunned our entire town. During that tough time, Clint stepped in and took responsibility for every detail. He didn't simply give instructions or delegate tasks; instead, he personally supported the family, walking them through each step of the process.

Mulligan leaned forward.

"He found the right church — one that could hold what felt like half the county. Went with the family. Stood beside them. Same thing at the cemetery. Walked the grounds with them and helped them choose the spot where their husband and father would rest.

Mulligan's tail slowed.

"The fire department stayed with him — rotating honor guard — twenty -four hours a day, even through Christmas. Clint was there on Christmas Day, making sure every detail was right. Every chair. Every flower."

I paused.

"At the graveside, the widow asked him if she could have roses for her and the kids to place on the casket."

Mulligan's ears lifted.

"He already had them. I looked over, and Clint was on one knee, handing each child a rose — one at a time — talking to them quietly like nothing else in the world mattered."

I took a breath.

"That," I said, "is the finest thing I've seen in fifty years of funeral service."

Mulligan nodded once. Slow. Serious.

"Boss, that's not a funeral director. That's a guardian."

"Arnold's eleven," I said. "Plays every sport known to mankind. He and Clint are champion wake surfers — six years running."

"I can't surf," Mulligan said. "But I do an excellent doggy paddle."

"And Amelia," I said, "is six going on sixteen. Sweet as sugar. She'll fall in love with Georgette at first sight. But she's also a bit of a cat person."

Mulligan froze.

"A cat person?"

"Her other grandparents have cats," I said. "She can't have one because Arnold's allergic."

Mulligan nodded gravely. "We'll win her over. I'll bring charm. Georgette will bring cheekbones."

Family Arrives

The back gate creaked, and Clint's voice called, "You got room for one more herd?"

Arnold burst through first, football in hand, grinning like he owned the place. Amelia followed, clutching a stuffed kitten and walking Jack, their Jack Russell, who immediately darted toward the ball launcher, barking like he was auditioning for demolition duty.

"Dad," Clint said, giving me a quick hug, "what's this contraption?"

"State -of -the -art funeral home fitness equipment," I said. "Mulligan's idea."

Before Clint could reply, Mulligan stepped forward, offered a polite nod, and said, "Evening, Director Sheridan. You must be the prodigy."

Clint blinked. "He talks?"

"Told you," I said.

Dinner turned into a small festival. The kids chased tennis balls. Jack chased the kids. Mulligan operated the ball launcher like a maestro, nose-pressing buttons and calling out, "heads up!" with alarming authority.

Fa nearly dropped her tea when one ball ricocheted off the grill lid. "That thing's a lawsuit waiting to happen!"

Dane laughed so hard she had to dab her eyes. Georgette sat beside her, composed and serene, leaning her head gently against Dane's knee now and then, like punctuation.

When the burgers were gone, and the fireflies came out, Arnold collapsed into a lawn chair. "Grandpa," he said, breathless, "this is the best night ever."

I looked around — my son, my grandkids, my wife, my sister, my ninety-six-year-old mother-in-law glowing under the string lights — and thought, he's right.

The Legend of Jefe (Family Edition)

"So, Mulligan," Arnold said, ever curious, "how did you learn to talk?"

I saw it — that gleam. Showtime.

"Well," Mulligan began, smoothing his fur, "it all started when I was owned by a rather unpleasant fellow named Jefe…"

The story went downhill — and uphill — from there.

When the last citronella candle sputtered out, the family packed up to go. Mulligan and Georgette lay side by side on the porch, watching taillights disappear.

"Good crowd," Mulligan said.

"You did well," I told him.

He wagged. "Every audience teaches you something. That boy's got courage. That girl's got imagination."

I laughed. "She kind of does."

Mulligan yawned. "Tomorrow, you should introduce me to your men's club."

"You want to go to the club?"

"Absolutely. I've got stories that pair well with cigars and bad domino hands."

He settled his chin on his paws. "Besides, those fellas sound like they could use a little hope."

I leaned back, the night soft around us, and thought maybe he was right.

Chapter 17 — Night at the Club (The Men of Mitzvah)

The Fort Worth Golf Club has a way of smoothing the day out like a well-oiled putter. You walk through the door and the air changes — less city, more country-club time warp.

It's a man-only place, sure, but it's where I go to unwind, trade bad jokes for worse advice, and, if the night's right, get roasted until I'm well done.

That evening, I walked in with Mulligan and Georgette at my side, as if we were bringing live entertainment.

The usual suspects were already at our table — the same fellows who showed up rain or shine, mischief in their eyes and stories on their lips. We call ourselves the Men of Mitzvah, mainly because someone thought it sounded respectable, and the rest of us didn't bother to argue.

Mac runs the games and the scores. He's the one who always gets the tee times and organizes the golf. At the head of the long table sat Mac, the picture of smug competence, and surrounding him was the domino gang:

Harvey "Hacksaw" Johnson, who cheats with confidence.

Mike "Birdie" Callahan, who grumbles about line calls like a referee.

Bill "Bitcher" Sampson, who tells the best stories two wines in.

And Moe "Shuffle" Rosen, who could stack tiles in his sleep.

The domino table was a religion, and those boys worshipped loudly.

"Cole!" Mac called out with that grin that's more invitation than insult. "You brought the circus."

I set the leash down and let Mulligan trot ahead. The room did what it always does — a dozen good-natured looks, a dozen rolled eyes, and then the pitchfork of obligation: ribbing.

Mac didn't waste time. "Well, I'll be—what's that? You bringing home a hedge?"

He lifted his glass of scotch.

Mulligan cocked an ear. "Mac, in that voice that commands attention in rooms and airports alike, "next time you call me ugly, I'll bite your ass."

The table froze.

Mac laughed first. Then the rest of them roared.

"He talks!"

"He talks!"

"What else you got, Cole — is he doing taxes next?"

Mulligan sat, chest proud, and began.

He always starts with Jefe — the bad choices, the double life — but tonight he gave the familiar opener a new twist.

"When I was a pup," Mulligan said, "Jefe's life was… complicated. One night, shots rang out at his place. I ran like the devil was after me and didn't stop until I collapsed under a tree out on a ridge."

The men leaned in.

"I woke up next to a marker that read Hanging Tree — funny name for a place that's really a golf course. Downtown Fort Worth spread out below like somebody's model train set."

They knew where this was going.

"There was a man hitting balls," Mulligan continued. "He had a boy out there catching them on the first bounce and dropping them into a bag. The boy was a disaster — clumsy as a newborn colt. The man kept yelling, 'On the first bounce! On the first bounce!' The kid kept missing."

Harvey snorted and nearly spilled his drink. "Sounds like my grandson at Christmas."

"I couldn't take it anymore," Mulligan said. "I ran out, started catching the balls myself. Dropped them right into the bag. The man came over, looked me up and down like he'd just found something he'd lost in the couch cushions, and said, 'Son, I could use someone like you on this range.'"

Mulligan paused.

"I asked, 'What does it pay?' He told me a name I'd only heard whispered in legends — Ben Hogan. Said he'd call me Shaggy."

The room went quiet.

"That's the full story," Mulligan said. "I wasn't just a shag dog. I was Ben Hogan's shag boy and caddie. He taught me how to read the wind, respect the turf, and always wear a hat."

"Ben Hogan?" Mac barked. "You are pulling our leg?"

Mulligan wagged once. "Ask anyone who's played Shady Oaks. He taught me dignity — and the danger of approach shots."

Mac stood and adopted his best announcer's voice. "So, Cole, if he's Hogan's shag boy, can he fix my slice?"

Mulligan fixed him with a look. "Maybe, Mac. But next time someone calls me ugly—" he nodded toward Mac's scotch, "— they'll need something stronger than a mulligan."

The table exploded.

The dominoes were forgotten for a while. Birdie slid a tile toward Mulligan, who sniffed it with the seriousness of a wine critic.

The questions came fast.

Did he take tips?

Could he change a tire?

How many languages did he speak?

"Two," Mulligan said. "Dog and sarcasm."

Georgette accepted a napkin placed on a chair and looked politely bored by the whole affair.

At some point, Harvey stood and raised his glass.

"To Cole — for bringing the best entertainment this club's seen since Callahan wore a kilt. To Mulligan — for being uglier than any of us and still having more charm. And to Mac — may your slice forever find the rough."

"May your divots be small and your putts kinder," the group answered.

Later, the domino players returned to the table. Saul rapped his knuckles on the wood.

"You want in, mutt?" he asked. "We'll let you shuffle if you don't eat the tiles."

Mulligan nodded solemnly. "I promise to be mostly well-behaved. But I reserve the right to wag when the stakes are high."

By the end of the night, Mulligan had earned a tiny pile of chips, kissed the best tile for luck, and secured a permanent seat at our table — not as a member (rules are rules), but as an honorary mascot and favorite running joke.

On the walk to the car, Mac clapped me on the shoulder. "You know, he's alright. Ugly or not — he's alright."

Mulligan hopped into the truck like a man who'd found his pew. Georgette settled beside him, calm and composed.

"You did well tonight," I told him.

He stuck his head out the window and sniffed the night air. "Cole, tonight we taught a room full of grown men how to laugh at a new story. Tomorrow, we will teach them how to cry with honesty. One day at a time."

Mac's voice trailed after us. "Next week, bring him a cigar. And maybe a vest."

Mulligan closed his eyes. "Only if it's for show. I prefer biscuits."

We drove home under the lamplight, the club shrinking behind us and the long Texas night stretching ahead — a little softer than when we'd arrived.

The Men of Mitzvah would have something else to tell on Monday.

And riding home, it struck me that maybe that's the whole point.

Small miracles, told well, don't just pass the time.

They make a life worth living.

Chapter 18 — Marketing Mayhem

By Thursday morning, Mulligan had officially declared himself our new Director of Community Engagement.

Fa said that sounded suspiciously like trouble in a bow tie.

Clint was in the conference room with his laptop open, planning our next advertising push — billboards, digital spots, something fresh to remind people that Sheridan Funeral Homes weren't just another funeral home.

Mulligan hopped onto a chair beside him, paws on the table like a furry executive.

"Clint, you're doing this all wrong. People don't want marketing. They want meaning. We need a story."

Clint smiled, humoring him. "All right, genius. What's your story?"

He leaned back, eyes half-closed like a CEO on a vision quest.

"Life Is Ruff — Celebrate It Well."

Fa nearly dropped her coffee. "Lord help us, the dog's got a slogan."

Mulligan began pacing the room like Don Draper on four legs.

"Think multimedia. Podcast. Social posts. Outreach. We'll call the podcast Six Feet Above — good stories from people who've loved well and lost well."

Clint's eyebrows lifted. "That's… actually good."

"Of course it is," Mulligan said. "We interview families, hospice nurses, maybe even the janitor who finds the lost umbrellas. Everyone's got a sermon hiding in their pocket."

Georgette gave a soft, supportive woof and wagged her pom-pom tail.

Clint pulled up a few mockups on her screen. "We've been thinking about photos of sunlight through the chapel windows."

Mulligan jumped down. "Too expected. Show the life around the place — coffee brewing, kids chasing a ball in the parking lot, laughter sneaking out between services. People don't fear death; they fear being forgotten. Show them we remember."

Fa crossed her arms, then nodded. "He's not wrong."

Mulligan grinned. "Exactly. For the tagline video, I suggest we feature my associate, Ms. Georgette.

He paused for effect.

"Cut to: Georgette in pearls, sitting beside a mahogany casket like she's on the cover of Southern Living."

Fa screamed. "Not on the velvet!"

Mulligan waved her off. "Relax, Fa. It's tastefully tragic."

Once the laughter settled, Mulligan trotted over to the whiteboard.

"Here's where we stop selling and start serving, writing in block letters: HOSPICE VISITS.

"We go once a week. Comfort families, staff, and anyone who needs a tail wag more than a therapy session. I'm told I'm excellent at listening."

He cleared his throat.

"Here are my ideas."

One: Children's Hospital.

"Remember that little girl who wouldn't talk until I whispered to her? I want to go back. Maybe she will read me a story this time."

Two: Presbyterian Night Shelter.

"Full circle. I owe them. Blankets, socks, maybe some of Fa's banana bread. I'll give a short talk about hope and the art of chasing what you can't yet see."

Fa sighed. "I knew that banana bread would come back to haunt me."

Three: Podcast Launch.

"Six Feet Above. Tagline: Where the stories live on. I want guests who've turned loss into laughter. People like us."

He stepped back, satisfied.

"Visionary," Clint said.

"Raccoon," Mulligan corrected. "But visionary raccoon."

Clint couldn't resist. "Let's test your slogan. We'll film a quick spot."

He set up his phone before anyone could object. Moments later, Mulligan and Georgette were standing in the chapel, haloed by stained glass.

Mulligan faced the camera.

"At Sheridan Funeral Homes, we don't just honor lives — we celebrate them. Because every story deserves a good laugh, a good cry, and a good dog."

Fa groaned. "We're going to get letters."

By the next morning, the clip had 22,000 views and a comment section full of heart emojis.

Julia looked at me over her coffee. "He's either a genius or a menace."

"Both," I said. "And I think he just paid for next month's ad budget."

Evening Reflection

That night, the house felt alive again — phones buzzing, laughter drifting down the hall.

Mulligan lay by my chair. Teddy sprawled between my legs, tail thumping.

"You really think people want to hear stories about funerals?" I asked.

Mulligan yawned. "No, boss. They want love stories that won't quit. That's what a good funeral is — proof somebody mattered."

Julia smiled. "So, what's next, Director Mulligan?"

He tilted his head toward the window, city lights glowing beyond the glass.

"We start small. Hospice tomorrow. Shelter next week. The stories will find us."

Anna Belle sighed contentedly. Teddy barked once in his sleep. Georgette rested her chin on Dane's knee, eyes full of quiet devotion.

For a long moment, nobody spoke.

Then Mulligan whispered, "For twenty dollars, I'd say this is turning into quite the investment."

The next morning, I caught him rummaging through my golf bag.

"What are you doing?" I asked.

"Packing for my debut at the Fort Worth Golf Club."

"You don't golf."

"No," Mulligan grinned, "but I putt on purpose."

I should've known right then.

Marketing Mayhem was just getting started.

Chapter 19 — A Visit to Remember

Fa caught me in the hallway one Tuesday morning, coffee in one hand and the schedule in the other.

"Cole," she said, "Mrs. Ellison's daughter called. Her mom's in hospice. She asked if you could stop by."

Before I could answer, Mulligan lifted his head from under my desk.

"I'd like to tag along, 'I have exceptional bedside manners and a calming scent profile."

Fa smirked. "You sure it's not the bacon you rolled in this morning?"

"Ma'am," Mulligan replied, "some call it cologne."

So that afternoon, Mulligan and I loaded into the Suburban. Georgette rode elegantly in the backseat, like she was headed to tea with the Queen.

Hospice rooms always have a kind of holy stillness, the kind that asks you to whisper even when no one's told you to.

Mrs. Ellison lay by the window, her breathing shallow, her daughter seated beside her, fingers laced tight in her lap.

Mulligan padded forward and did something I'll never forget.

He didn't talk.

He climbed onto the foot of the bed, curled into a tight loaf, and rested his chin gently on Mrs. Ellison's blanket.

The room seemed to exhale.

For the first time in days, Mrs. Ellison opened her eyes. She smiled faintly, reached a trembling hand toward Georgette—who had quietly come to stand beside Mulligan—and whispered, "George."

"That was my mama's poodle's name," the daughter said softly.

Georgette pressed her nose into Mrs. Ellison's fingers. A small sigh escaped the woman's lips—half laughter, half release.

After a while, Mrs. Ellison's daughter said quietly, "Mama hasn't spoken in three days."

Mulligan nodded solemnly. "Sometimes heaven sends advance notice."

The daughter froze. "Did he just—?"

I cut in gently. "He does that."

When we left the room, her daughter was silent. Out in the sunlight, she finally said, "That dog's a messenger."

Mulligan stretched, tail swishing. "Ma'am, I just deliver comfort in small, furry installments."

But I noticed the way he looked back through the window—serious, almost reverent.

We didn't talk much on the drive home.

Halfway down Camp Bowie, Mulligan cleared his throat.

"You know, that lady… she said 'George.' I think she saw someone waiting on the porch for her."

I glanced over. "You think dogs wait, too?"

"Cole," he said softly, "the good ones always do."

That night, after supper, Julia set two Dr Peppers on the porch rail—one for her, one for the dog who used to burp after every sip.

Mulligan sat beside her without a word.

Dane joined them, her Bible tucked under one arm. She looked down at Georgette. "You remind me so much of my old George."

Georgette wagged delicately and laid her head in Dane's lap.

Inside, I stood at the kitchen sink, looking through the window. The scene was so still, so right, I didn't want to break it.

Mulligan turned his head slightly and caught my eye.

"Cole," he said quietly, "today wasn't about funerals. It was about remembering we're not done helping."

Later, as I locked up for the night, Mulligan was already sprawled on the rug, tail thumping lazily.

"Tomorrow, I've got an idea for a new outreach."

I groaned. "Please tell me it doesn't involve TikTok."

He grinned. "Better. Golf. Therapy. Think about it—forty acres of manicured lawn and a captive audience of men in need of humility."

I shook my head, smiling. "You're impossible."

"Maybe," he said, eyes closing, "but impossible's where miracles hide."

Chapter 20 — The Golf Club Incident

(or "Fore! and Fur")

Saturday mornings at the Fort Worth Golf Club are a kind of ritual. Part church, part circus, and part confession.

There are twenty of us who play every week. Same faces. Same jokes. Same lies about handicaps. The bets aren't high, but the bragging rights are pure gold.

Mundo, my oldest friend, and I were paired together—partners against every other two-man team. Mundo's been my running buddy, drinking buddy, and voice of reason since before I had any reason to listen.

That morning, though, we had a new team member.

"Cole," Mundo said as I pulled into the lot, "tell me you didn't bring a dog with you."

Mulligan popped his head out the window, sunglasses on, tongue out.

"The name's Mulligan—ironically enough. You could say golf was my destiny."

By the time we reached the first tee, the banter was already flying.

Mac—who treats every round like the final day at Augusta—looked at the dog and said,

"You brought the ugly one as he puffed on a cigar the size of a Slim Jim."

Mulligan's low growl vibrated through the bag straps.

I whispered, "Behave."

He sat up straighter. "Fine. But I'm keeping score."

Bitch—real name Richard, nickname earned—already two glasses of wine in said.

"Hope that dog doesn't bark during my swing."

"I never bark," Mulligan said quietly. "I only heckle."

Hole One

Mac teed up. Waggle-waggle. Deep breath.

As his backswing rose, Mulligan muttered just loud enough for the gallery of oak trees to hear,

"Looks like he's digging a trench, not hitting a ball."

Mac sliced it deep into the trees.

Mundo bent double, laughing. "You jinxed him!"

I hissed, "Stop it, or you're going back in the cart."

Mulligan folded his paws. "Just providing color commentary."

Hole Three

By the third hole, the day had turned into pure Texas spring—sun high, breeze lazy, tempers loosening.

Mac set his cigar on the ground before his shot.

The moment his back was turned, Mulligan trotted over, sniffed once, and lifted a leg.

I didn't even have time to stop him.

Mac swung, turned, picked up the cigar, and stuck it back in his mouth.

One puff later, he froze.

"Cole," he said slowly, "your dog's got issues."

Mundo wheezed, half-crying with laughter.

Mulligan shrugged. "That's what he gets for calling me ugly."

Hole Nine

Somewhere around the turn, I found my rhythm.

Every time I sank a long putt, Mulligan danced—front paws up, tail spinning like a propeller.

Players from other groups started cheering.

"Cole and Mulligan—minus five!" someone shouted.

Mulligan bowed. "It's all in the hips, gentlemen."

By the eighteenth hole, Mundo and I had beaten Mac and Bitch and taken the side bets.

A clean sweep.

Mulligan strutted beside me like a prizefighter leaving the ring.

"Admit it, I'm good luck."

"You're lucky I don't get banned," I muttered.

Inside, the twenty of us gathered to settle up—stacks of bills, louder lies.

Mac paid out with a grimace. "You owe the mutt a cut."

Mulligan leaned on a barstool. "I accept payment in sliders and bourbon."

Then—because he can't help himself—he launched into jokes.

"You ever notice golfers are the only people who celebrate digging holes they'll never fill?"

The room cracked up.

He had a dozen ones like that—one-liners sharp enough to slice a Pro-V1.

By the end, even Mac was laughing.

He raised his glass. "To the ugliest good-luck charm we've ever seen."

Mulligan wagged. "I'll drink to that—but make mine water with a twist of lime."

Back in the truck, Mulligan leaned against the window, pleased with himself.

"I think I made an impression."

"Oh, you did," I said. "On Mac's cigar, his ego, and the entire men's association."

He grinned. "So, when do we play again?"

"Not for a while," I said. "Club rules might need rewriting first."

He chuckled. "Good. Gives me time to work on my short game—and my stand -up act."

He tilted his head toward the horizon.

"You know, boss, laughter and golf have a lot in common."

"How's that?"

"Both prove grace is real—because nobody deserves to have that much fun after that many bad shots."

I laughed all the way home.

That night, Julia asked how it went.

Before I could answer, Mulligan said,

"Let's just say, boss here finally learned what a real mulligan feels like."

Julia laughed until she cried—the kind of laugh that sounded like healing.

And I thought, maybe that's what this whole adventure is about.

Chapter 21 — Back to the Beginning

Mulligan was sprawled under my desk one morning, paws twitching as if he were chasing something noble in his dreams, when he suddenly sat up and said, "Boss, it's time we did a little good."

I peered over my coffee. "You already do plenty. You've revived our spirits, improved our cardio, and personally lowered my blood pressure by at least five points."

He wagged. "Not that kind of good. The big kind. The kind that smells like disinfectant and hope."

Julia peeked in from the kitchen. "If that's what I think it is, I'll pack water bowls and tissues."

Georgette looked up from her perfectly curled paws, gave a low, elegant bark, and tilted her head toward the car keys. She already knew.

We were going back to the Children's Hospital—where Georgette had once been a therapy dog—and to the Presbyterian Night Shelter, where Mulligan had once found both hunger and grace.

The automatic doors slid open with a soft sigh, as if the building itself were relieved to see old friends.

A nurse at the front desk blinked, then gasped. "Georgette? Mulligan? Oh Lord—someone call the playroom. Tell them the angels are back!"

Georgette walked in like she was gliding on air—head high, tail a question mark of grace.

Mulligan trotted beside her, wearing the kind of grin that could make even a ventilator hum a little brighter.

In the hallway, a young nurse whispered, "That's her. That's the poodle who used to visit before she got adopted."

When we reached the pediatric wing, the air changed. You could feel it—soft, expectant, like a church just before the first hymn.

"Would you like to say hello?" I asked.

Mulligan cleared his throat. "Would I?" Then, to the kids, "hello, esteemed humans. We come bearing fur, affection, and absolutely no copays."

Laughter—pure and unfiltered—bubbled across the room.

A small girl in a pink cap whispered, "I remember her."

She reached out a trembling hand, and Georgette leaned forward, resting her chin gently on the girl's wrist.

"She remembers you, too," Julia said softly.

In the corner, a boy with a bandaged leg looked up. "Do you really talk?"

Mulligan winked. "Only when it's worth saying something."

"Say something funny," the boy said.

Mulligan thought for a moment, then replied, "Never trust a cat who says they're vegan."

The boy laughed so hard his monitor started beeping, and two nurses came running—until they saw why.

Everyone was smiling.

We spent the afternoon moving from room to room.

Georgette worked like a quiet symphony—curling beside sleeping children, pressing gently against the ones who were afraid.

Mulligan, ever the orator, told abridged versions of his Jefe adventures—light on the crime, heavy on the comedy.

By the time we left, half the floor was giggling, and the other half was asking if they could keep the dogs.

One nurse wiped her eyes. "You two gave them more than medicine ever could."

Georgette turned her head, regal and humble at once.

Mulligan looked back and said, "Miracles don't always wear scrubs."

The Presbyterian Night Shelter

By evening, the sun bled into the horizon, and downtown shimmered gold.

The shelter stood sturdy against the shadows, its doors already open.

"Mulligan!" called the director, a man with kind eyes and calloused hands. "And you brought your better half!"

Georgette gave a polite woof. Mulligan bowed like a visiting dignitary.

They led us first to the Women's and Children's Building—the place Mulligan had once called home. The same hallway where he'd curled up on cold tile years ago, now brighter, cleaner, warmer.

Some of the residents remembered him.

"You're the dog who used to walk the halls at night," one woman said. "Keeping us company."

Mulligan nodded solemnly. "And you're the lady who made the world's best peanut butter sandwich. I still dream about it."

Laughter filled the room.

Georgette padded over to a small boy sitting on the floor and gently dropped one of her favorite toys—a faded stuffed duck—at his feet. He looked up, surprised, then hugged her neck.

The director stepped forward, holding something behind his back. "We found this when we were cleaning out storage. Thought you should have it."

He handed me a small, hand-painted ceramic dog bowl.

Around the rim, in wobbly letters, it read:

For Mulligan — Our Hero

The paint had faded, but the love hadn't.

"The kids made it for him years ago," the director said. "Before… before he was sold off. They never got to give it to him."

I looked down at Mulligan. His tail was still. His eyes glistened.

He sniffed the bowl once, then said quietly, "Guess I finally came home."

The room went silent.

Then someone started clapping.

Then everyone was clapping.

Even Georgette let out a happy bark that sounded a lot like Amen.

By the time we pulled into the driveway, twilight had melted into starlight.

Inside, the house was warm and humming—Dane reading in her chair, the faint smell of coffee still in the air.

Anna Belle appeared from the hallway, tail wagging, a bag of unpopped popcorn clutched proudly in her mouth.

Julia laughed. "I think she's saying it's movie night."

Teddy barked once in agreement, his tail sweeping like a broom.

So, we popped the corn, dimmed the lights, and let the dogs choose the movie.

Mulligan studied the options and said, "Old Yeller. Everyone needs a good cry now and then."

"Are you sure?" Julia asked. "That one breaks hearts."

"That's the point," he said. "It means they still work."

We watched together—dogs and people, paw and hand—sharing popcorn, tears, and silence.

When the ending came, Dane dabbed her eyes. "I forgot how sad that was."

Mulligan sighed softly. "Sad's not the same as broken. Sad means we loved right."

Georgette leaned against Dane's knee. Anna Belle lay her head in Julia's lap. Teddy's tail thumped against my shoe.

And in that quiet, I realized maybe that's what all this was about.

Not fixing what's gone—but learning to love what's still here.

The next morning, I found Mulligan and Georgette side by side at my desk, noses pressed to the computer screen.

On it was a document titled:

Operation: 10,000 Views — The Sheridan & Son Video Campaign

"Boss," Mulligan said, tail wagging, "you're going viral. Community outreach, therapy dog videos, hospice smiles—the works. You'll thank me later."

I rubbed my eyes. "And you're sure this won't get us banned from the internet?"

He winked. "Not unless we tell the Jefe story again."

Chapter 22 — The Pawdcast

It started, as most of our better ideas do, over coffee and mild chaos.

Clint was at his desk, surrounded by sticky notes that read things like Heartfelt, not sappy, and Less taxidermy humor.

Mulligan sat in my office chair, scrolling through YouTube like a dog on a mission.

I was trying to understand why we'd received three phone calls asking when our podcast would be released, even though none of us had agreed to that yet.

"Dad," Clint said, tapping his pen, "your last community video hit over six thousand views. People loved it—the dogs, the humor, the kindness. They said it made them feel good about life again. So... we're doing a podcast."

"Or," Mulligan said without looking up, "as I prefer to call it— a Pawdcast. Spelled with a W, obviously. Branding, people."

Clint looked up from his desk. "He's been workshopping names all morning. My favorite so far was Dead Serious with Mulligan."

"Too dark," Julia said.

"Too accurate," Mulligan replied.

I sighed. "All right. If we're really doing this, it must sound like us. A little humor, a little heart, and a whole lot of respect. We're talking about grief here—not golf."

Mulligan nodded solemnly. "Got it. Humor with halos."

Setting the Stage

We cleared out the small reception room next to the chapel and turned it into a makeshift studio.

Fa found some old church pew cushions that doubled as sound panels. Larry hung a thick black curtain to soften the echo. And Julia—bless her organized heart—borrowed a microphone from TCU broadcasting.

"You can't have a Pawdcast without paws," Mulligan declared.

The plan was simple: record one long session, break it into segments, and post it across both of our funeral homes' pages—Guy Sheridan and Cole Sheridan & Son.

Each episode would focus on one theme: heritage, community, loss, and celebration—the same values we try to live out every day.

Before we started, I gathered everyone in the chapel.

"Remember," I said, "this is about helping people feel seen. We can laugh, but it has to come from love. And for heaven's sake, keep Mulligan from hijacking the intro."

Recording Day

The "ON AIR" sign was a sticky note Fa had drawn with a red marker, but it worked.

Mulligan hopped onto his stool, cleared his throat, and announced, "Testing. Testing. Woof. You're listening to The Sheridan Story: Paws, Purpose, and the People We Serve. I'm Mulligan—part-time grief counselor, full-time genius."

"Cut," I said immediately.

He blinked. "What? I'm setting the tone."

Clint laughed from behind the soundboard. "Tone achieved."

So, we began—and just like that, it clicked.

The dogs sat still, Georgette regal beside Mulligan. Julia read her questions like a pro. Clint kept us grounded. And I did my best to sound wiser than I felt.

Below is what went out into the world that day—the first episode of The Sheridan Story.

🎙️ "Paws, Purpose, and the People We Serve"

(The Pawdcast — Episode 1)

Cole:

Welcome to The Sheridan Story, where we talk about faith, family, and the funny ways compassion shows up—sometimes with muddy paws.

I'm Cole Sheridan, joined by my son Clint, my wife Julia, and the dog who started this circus—Mulligan.

Mulligan:

Circus? Please. I prefer Ministry of Mirth.

Julia:

We're recording this from our chapel—the same place where families laugh, cry, and remember the people they love.

Today we're talking about heritage, community, loss, and celebration—the heart of who we are at Sheridan Funeral Homes.

Clint:

That's Guy Sheridan and Cole Sheridan & Son—two homes, one mission: to serve people the way we'd want to be served.

Cole:

Our family's been doing this for more than a hundred years. But lately, something's changed.

Turns out compassion walks on four legs.

Mulligan:

And occasionally talks back.

(Laughter)

Julia:

We've seen how animals break through walls, grief builds. Sometimes a tail wag says what words can't.

That's what this show is about: finding light in hard places and sharing hope, one story at a time.

Mulligan:

Also snacks. Never forget snacks.

Cole:

Stick around. If you're grieving, healing, or need a reminder that laughter and loss can share the same space—this is for you.

(Outro music fades)

The Second Pawdcast — "Laughter in the Hard Places"

We recorded a second episode that same afternoon. Momentum has a way of sneaking up on you.

"This one's important," Mulligan said. "People need to know it's okay to laugh again. We're not selling grief—we're offering hope with a grin."

Julia rolled her eyes but hit Record.

Mulligan:

"Sometimes people ask if laughter disrespects the dead. I tell them the opposite—it's proof love's still alive."

Cole:

That's true. You can't laugh if your heart's closed.

Mulligan:

And if you can't laugh, you're probably constipated.

Julia dropped her pen. "Cut."

"Leave it," I said. "People will relate."

From there, the episode softened.

Clint talked about families bringing photo albums to arrangements—laughter through tears, stories that kept people alive a little longer.

I shared one about a gentleman who left a note in his will that read, play 'Take Me Out to the Ballgame' and pass out Cracker Jacks.

The episode ended with Mulligan's voice, low and sincere.

"Grief doesn't ask you to forget. It just asks you to remember differently."

Even Fa sat quietly for a long moment.

After the Pawdcast

When the microphones went silent, the room stayed warm—the good kind of quiet.

"You know, Dad," Clint said, exhaling, "that actually felt good."

"It was good," Julia said. "It was honest. That's what people will connect with."

Fa poked her head in. "I don't know who your agent is, Mulligan, but you're a natural."

He stretched, smug. "Darling, I'm just here to make grief glamorous."

I scratched behind his ear. "You did good, buddy. All of you did."

Late afternoon light spilled through the stained glass.

For the first time in a long while, the building didn't just look alive—it felt alive.

Mulligan hopped into a pew and looked up at the window. "Cole," he said quietly, "I think this place finally found its voice."

I smiled. "You mean our voice."

He wagged. "Same thing."

That night, Julia played the Pawdcast on her iPad while Georgette snoozed at her feet.

When Mulligan heard his own voice through the speaker, he sighed like an artist admiring his masterpiece.

Then, almost to himself, he said,

"Tomorrow, Cole… tomorrow's a harder kind of story. One where laughter meets loss again."

Chapter 23 — Sunny Day

The phone rang just after breakfast, that kind of ring that somehow already feels heavy before you even pick it up.

"Cole," the voice said softly, "it's Mary Bill's wife. Sunny passed away last night."

I didn't say anything for a moment. There are calls I've taken thousands of times in my life, but this one went straight through me.

"Thank you for letting me know," I finally managed. "When would you like to come in?"

"Today," she said. "We'd like you to handle everything. Bill would've wanted it that way."

When I hung up, Mulligan was sitting in the doorway, head tilted.

"Bad news?"

I nodded. "One of my best friends. His name was Bill Day—but everyone called him Sunny."

Mulligan's ears perked. "Good name for a man who must've brought light."

"Yeah," I said quietly. "That's exactly who he was."

Remembering Sunny

I sat down across from Mulligan and just started talking—the talking that doesn't need a plan.

"Mulligan, I've had more fun with his name than any man deserves. I'd call him Partly Cloudy when he was in a mood. Once, he told me he was my 'forecast for trouble and that my jokes were sick.' I'd laugh, and he'd say, 'You really are sick, Cole.' That's how he ended every joke I ever told him—and I told him plenty of jokes.

Mulligan smiled faintly. "Sounds like you two spoke fluent nonsense and loyalty."

"That's about right," I said. "He was my banker—and never said no, even when he should have. We played golf together, went on trips, ran the Chamber, swapped presidencies like bad habits. Every Tuesday was poker night at his place. Sometimes it ended when the sun came up. Always the same—laughter, barbecue, tall tales, nobody keeping score but him.

"He was the kind of man who looked out for everyone around him—made sure the fun never went too far, the golf never got too serious, and the laughs never ran out."

Mulligan lowered his head. "Sounds like the kind of man heaven didn't want to wait for."

"Yeah," I said, my voice catching. "He was also the guy I'd call if I didn't want to eat lunch alone. The one who picked up the phone, no questions asked. I love what I do, Mulligan—but damn it, I hate doing it today."

He stepped closer and rested a paw on my knee. "Then let me help carry it, boss."

A Celebration, not a Goodbye

That afternoon, I sat at my desk sketching the service. I could already see it—the Guy Sheridan Chapel filled to the doors, sunlight spilling through the windows as if trying to make more room.

His golf clubs would stand beside his picture. On the table, a deck of cards—the ten, jack, queen, and king of spades facing up. The fifth card is face down.

Stacey would draw it—just one of the aces. Nobody would look. We'd place the other three in his casket to be cremated with him.

If I knew Sunny, that hidden card was the ace of spades. He'd drawn more royal flushes than anyone I'd ever met, and he never bragged too much.

By late afternoon, his wife and daughters came in.

Mulligan and Georgette waited quietly in the corner—tails still, eyes soft. You could feel the weight of their love for him in every pause between words.

They told stories—how he'd helped neighbors during the freeze, how he never missed a ballgame, how he'd leave notes that said, Smile. It's a good day. It's a Sunny Day.

When they finished, I promised them we'd make this perfect—not polished, but Bill -perfect.

That Evening

After they left, I sat alone in the chapel.

The pews were empty, but somehow the air wasn't.

Mulligan came and sat beside me.

"You going to speak?" he asked.

"I don't know if I can," I said. "I want to. I don't want anyone else to. But I don't know if I can do it without falling apart."

He leaned against my leg. "Then fall apart, Cole. That's what friends are for—even the ones listening from heaven."

Three days later, sunlight poured through the chapel glass in wide, quiet bands. The chairs were set, the flowers placed, the music ready.

I stood in the doorway, hands folded, looking out over what would soon be a celebration—not a goodbye.

Mulligan sat beside me, eyes bright.

"He's already here, boss," he said softly. "I can feel the warmth."

I nodded. "Yeah," I whispered. "A Sunny Day."

Chapter 24 — Sunny's Funeral

On the day of Sunny's funeral, I was a little irritable—and nervous.

I've been doing this for fifty years, and I want every funeral to be perfect. But I found myself wanting this one to be especially perfect.

I had agreed to speak, and I was having a hard time staying composed.

A few hours before the service, I slipped into the chapel alone to settle my thoughts.

Up front stood Sunny's golf bag, leaning proudly beside a table with his picture and five cards laid out neatly: the ten, jack, queen, and king of spades, with the fifth card turned face down.

In my heart, I knew it was the ace of spades—because Sunny had drawn more royal flushes than anyone I'd ever known.

Me? My number is still zero.

As I looked at his clubs, I smiled. For as successful as Sunny was—and as often as I think I need a new set every year—he was still playing the same ones he'd bought at least fifteen years ago.

A few of the photographs in the video tribute had him in a coat and tie. I only saw him dressed like that a handful of times, usually when I needed a loan for something nonessential, like a boat or another impractical idea.

The video tribute was rolling on the screen, set to his favorite country music.

I thought about all the rounds of golf we shared. I loved pulling up to the first tee with my speaker blasting rap music just to get his goat. Don't worry, I don't actually like rap. I'd switch it off quickly.

My mind drifted to the time the Dallas Cowboys opened their golf course, and Sunny and I took on Don and Stew.

Don and Stew were clearly better golfers, but the real challenge came after Sunny, and I somehow won our annual Boys' Trip Tournament at White Bluff—a lucky round if there ever was one.

This was before cart speakers and playlists. I had a boom box and managed to load individual songs for the round.

We let Don and Stew reach the first tee before us. Then Sunny and I rolled up behind them, blaring the Rocky theme.

Stew wasn't amused.

On the third hole—a par three over water—I queued up Splish Splash (I Was Taking a Bath) right as he swung. He promptly dumped the ball into the pond.

"You two can't beat us without gimmicks," he grumbled.

Sunny and I kept the soundtrack going and beat them one up on eighteen—more satisfying than winning the tournament the week before.

I watched the tribute video again—photos from tournaments, Chamber events, and Ambuc gatherings. Each one carried a memory.

In a few hours, the chapel would be filled with his friends—and mine. I wanted this to be a celebration.

I love his wife and his girls. Sunny loved them even more.

That's when Mulligan padded quietly into the chapel and sat beside me.

He looked up with those steady, coffee-colored eyes.

"You okay, boss?" he asked.

"Trying to be," I said.

"You've done this a thousand times," he said gently. "Why's this one different?"

"Because this one's for a man who helped make me who I am."

Mulligan settled in beside me. "Then let's make it count."

And somehow, that helped.

As people began to arrive, I noticed the mix—solemn faces, quiet smiles, nervous laughter.

The celebration was nearly ready in the chapel, and at two o'clock sharp, the minister from First Methodist stepped to the pulpit.

I couldn't tell you what he said or which hymn followed. I was too tight to hear it.

Then it was my turn.

Mulligan walked with me toward the podium.

"Just be yourself," he whispered.

For once, I listened.

"There's a poem I often use at funerals," I began. "It was written by Linda Ellis. It's called The Dash."

I paused.

"The poem talks about the dates on a headstone—the day someone is born, and the day they leave this world. But it says what really matters isn't either date."

"What matters is the small line between them—the dash."

"That dash represents everything that happened in between. The way someone lived. The way they loved. The way they treated others. The friendships they built. The difference they made."

"And when our time comes, it won't be about what we owned or what titles we held. It will be about how we spent our dash."

I looked out at the room.

"I've recited that poem at hundreds of funerals. And this is the part where I usually say, 'Sunny Day was born on this date and passed away on that date.'"

"But today, I'm not going to give you dates."

"Those numbers don't matter."

"What matters—the reason we're all here—is how he lived his dash."

"Twenty-seven years ago, I left my family business and went to Grapevine to start my own funeral home. I didn't know a soul."

"When the local paper ran a story about my opening, they interviewed the longtime mayor, who said, 'Grapevine already has two funeral homes that have been here over a hundred years. We didn't need another one, and I wish that building had stayed a restaurant.'"

"I read that and told Julia, 'Well, I don't think I'm getting a key to the city anytime soon.'"

"But we opened it anyway."

"One day, I went to a Chamber luncheon and saw an empty seat next to a guy with a familiar grin. I asked if I could sit there."

"He said, 'Sure.'"

"We talked. We found out we both loved golf. He asked how business was going."

"I told him, 'Growing pains.'"

"He said, 'What are you doing after this meeting? A few of us are heading to Grapevine Golf Course.'"

"I went—and had a blast."

"Sunny told me I should join Grapevine Ambucs. He said they did great things for kids with disabilities—and that the group was full of good men."

"He was right."

"From that day forward, Sunny included me in everything."

"I wouldn't have made it in Grapevine without him."

"On my fiftieth birthday, Julia took me on a cruise. We were out of contact for days."

"Just before we left, Sunny went into the hospital for what was supposed to be a minor surgery. I visited him the day before we sailed—he was in great spirits."

"What I didn't know was that complications followed, and Mary was told she might need to start thinking about final plans."

"But Sunny beat it."

"It took months. It changed things. But he never complained."

"And I know we were given more time with him because of that fight."

I paused, steadying myself.

"I wish I had a joke right now—but I don't."

"People come and go in our lives. Only a few come and stay forever."

"Sunny will stay with me forever."

After the Amen

When I stepped down, Mulligan was sitting beside me.

"Nice job," he said quietly.

"Thanks," I whispered. "You think he'd have liked it?"

"He'd have loved it," Mulligan said. "Especially the part where you admitted your handicap."

I laughed through the tears.

As the reception began, the laughter grew louder and the stories better.

Sunny would've approved.

And for the first time that day, I wasn't nervous anymore.

I was grateful.

Chapter 25 — One More Hole -in -One

A few weeks after Sunny's funeral, Mary allowed me to take some of his ashes to Grapevine Golf Course — the site of his only hole -in -one, on the seventh hole of the Mockingbird nine.

All the regulars were going to be there. Five foursomes. The same crew that had been teeing it up, talking trash, and telling lies for decades. We agreed that when we reached the seventh hole, everyone would stop, come over, and we'd put part of his ashes in the cup — give him one more ace for old time's sake.

Mulligan insisted on coming.

Georgette stayed home with Anna Belle and Teddy, which was probably for the best. Dane loved their company, and the house felt full when those three were holding court in the living room.

As we drove, the wind was already up — one of those gusty Texas days that'll slap your hat clean off your head and make you regret every loose paper you've ever owned.

"Mulligan," I said, "these are my old gang from Grapevine. The guys who helped make me who I am. I'm going to introduce you before the round, so go ahead and do your thing. Make it good. They'll dig it."

He perked up.

"And I don't care if you jack with them before, during, or after their swings," I added. "These are big boys. They can take it. They've given me enough grief over the years — it's about time they got some back."

He nodded solemnly, tongue hanging just a bit.

"Every one of these guys," I said, "helped me in more ways than I can tell you. If some things hadn't happened, I'd probably still be here — and I might've never met you."

Mulligan was quiet for a long time. Then he cleared his throat.

"I love you too, Boss."

I glanced over and could've sworn I saw a tear in his eye.

Or maybe it was just the wind.

The Clubhouse Introduction

When we pulled up to the clubhouse, the wind about blew us sideways. We headed inside for lunch before the round. The second I opened the door, all heads turned.

One of the guys grinned. "Looks like you brought emotional support, or did you finally lose enough bets to need a caddy that works for biscuits?"

"Both," I said.

Another one added, "You could've at least brought a good - looking dog. He looks like he's been through a dryer halfway through the cycle."

Before I could answer, Mulligan cleared his throat — loud enough to stop the room.

"Hi, I'm Mulligan. And for the record, I'm the one who taught him to play."

You could've heard a beer cap hit the floor.

Then the place exploded.

Mulligan launched straight into his origin story — starting with, "When I was a pup, I was owned by a bad guy named Jefe…" and rolling through cartels, the FBI, the CIA, and an "incident involving the Pope's schnauzer," before concluding:

"And that, gentlemen, is why I only play Titleist blessed by clergy."

They were crying, laughing.

"Who taught this dog to talk?" someone yelled.

"God," Mulligan said, "and the patience of this poor man beside me."

We teed off under a big Texas sky, the wind cutting across the fairways like a freight train. Mulligan rode shotgun in the cart, leaning into the turns like a retired greyhound.

By hole two, he was already running color commentary.

"Nice shot, Randy — if we're playing Find the Pond!"

"Careful, Jim. Winds got more hook than your mother-in-law's brisket!"

When someone chunked a chip, he howled, "You're supposed to hit the ball, not aerate the fairway!"

By the fourth hole, everyone wanted him in their cart.

When Stew stepped up to a par three over water, Mulligan gave me that look.

"You know what time it is, Boss?"

I nodded.

He hit play on my phone.

Splish Splash, I Was Taking a Bath echoed across the tee box.

Stew backed off, glared, regrouped — and promptly dumped it straight into the lake.

"You two are possessed," he muttered.

Mulligan wagged. "Just seasoned."

Hole Number Seven

When we reached number seven, everyone gathered — twenty men around the green, hats off, wind howling through the oaks.

Sunny's old foursome stood beside me as I knelt with the urn.

"He made his only ace here," I said. "So today, he gets another."

The wind surged just as I tried to pour. The ashes swirled, lifted, and scattered everywhere but the cup.

For half a second, the air went still.

Then Ron broke it.

"Hell, he had it over the hole and still couldn't make it!"

We lost it — laughter mixed with tears, the most memorable kind.

Mulligan looked skyward. "Nice try, pal. Winds got a mean slice today."

I brushed my hands together, grinning. "Well, at least he's officially part of the course now. And knowing Sunny, he'll be watching every bad swing from here to eternity."

After the Round

We finished eighteen with the usual mix of birdies, bogeys, and lies that grew bigger with every retelling.

Inside, bets were settled, stories swapped, and Mulligan held court near the bar, telling jokes so bad they somehow circled back around to funny.

At one point, he started singing Friends in Low Places — badly — until the bartender handed him a free beef stick to make it stop.

It was a perfect day: wind, laughter, and memories that didn't hurt quite as much anymore.

The Drive Home

On the ride home, Mulligan sprawled across the passenger seat, tongue out, ears flapping in the wind.

"Good day?" I asked.

He grinned. "Best funeral I've ever attended."

I laughed so hard I nearly missed my turn.

"Boss, I think we gave him what every golfer wants."

"What's that?"

"A second shot."

I smiled. "Yeah. And this one went straight down the middle."

He looked out the window, thoughtful. "Pretty windy, though."

"Yep."

"Think he'll still count it?"

I chuckled. "He always did."

Chapter 26 — America's Team, Heaven's Wish

It was a Tuesday morning when the call came in.

Fa answered first, then poked her head into my office with that look that says, you might want to take this one yourself.

"Cole," she said softly, "it's Wish with Wings."

Wish with Wings is one of those local miracles — a Fort Worth-based organization that's been granting wishes to children with life-threatening conditions since 1982. They don't make much noise, but what they do matters. Quietly. Deeply.

I picked up the phone.

"Mr. Sheridan," the woman said, "we have a special request — actually two. A little boy named Carter has cancer. He's ten years old. His wishes are to go to a Dallas Cowboys game… or to meet Mulligan and Georgette."

There was a pause.

"He saw your Pawdcast. It went viral. Carter's mom says he's watched it at least fifty times. He keeps saying, 'I want to meet the talking dog and the pretty one with the scarf.'"

For a moment, I couldn't speak.

I looked down at Mulligan, snoring softly beside my desk.

"Buddy," I whispered, "we've got a mission."

Wish with Wings reached out to the Cowboys. The story made its way up the ladder — all the way to Jerry Jones himself.

Now, I've heard every story there is about Jerry. But here's what I know for sure: the man has a heart big enough to fill AT&T Stadium twice over.

When they told him Carter's choice was "either a Cowboys game or Mulligan the talking dog," Jerry laughed and said, "Well, shoot — let's do both. The boy deserves the full show."

Not only did he invite Carter and his family to the game — he asked us too. Mulligan. Georgette. Julia. Me.

Then Jerry added, "Let's make it bigger. We'll dedicate the game to Wish with Wings, donate a million dollars, and challenge the fans to match it."

When I told Mulligan, he just stared at me.

"You're telling me, "He said slowly, "we're going to a Cowboys game?"

"Yes, sir."

He turned to Georgette. "Ma'am, fetch my finest collar. We're going to Jerry World."

AT&T Stadium was electric. You could feel eighty thousand people humming through the concrete.

Wish with Wings volunteers were everywhere — smiling, guiding, holding banners. They escorted us to Jerry's box, where Carter was waiting.

He was small. Pale. Wearing a Cowboys jersey three sizes too big — and a grin ten sizes too bright.

His mom sat beside him, tears never far from the surface, joy shining through them all.

When Mulligan trotted in, Carter's jaw dropped.

"He's real!"

Mulligan bowed. "At your service, young man."

Georgette followed, elegant as ever, her silk scarf fluttering.

Carter looked between them, wide-eyed. "You're even prettier than on TV!"

Mulligan leaned in and whispered, "Don't tell her that. Her ego's already in the Hall of Fame."

Carter laughed so hard he nearly spilled his Dr Pepper.

A few minutes later, Jerry Jones himself walked in, flashing that familiar grin.

"So, this is the young man who made us all step up our game."

He knelt beside Carter and shook his hand.

"You're the real MVP today."

Carter whispered, "I think Mulligan is."

Jerry winked. "Then I guess we'll share the spotlight."

Halftime: The Wish Heard 'Round the World

At halftime, they led us down to the field.

The jumbotron lit up:

THIS GAME IS DEDICATED TO CARTER —

AND TO ALL THE KIDS OF WISH WITH WINGS

The stadium roared — not a touchdown roar, something more profound.

Jerry took the microphone at the fifty-yard line.

"We're honored to be part of a little boy's dream — and to help keep dreams alive for so many others."

He held up a $1 million check made payable to Wish with Wings.

Then he smiled.

"But the real stars of the show are Carter, Mulligan, and Georgette."

The spotlight hit us.

Georgette gave a graceful bow.

Mulligan wagged his tail — and then, God help him, decided this was the perfect moment to howl the opening notes of the National Anthem.

The place exploded.

Players stopped warming up. Dak Prescott pointed and clapped. CeeDee Lamb laughed so hard he nearly dropped a ball.

Carter hugged Mulligan, and that dog pressed his nose to the boy's cheek.

"We're on your team now, kid," he whispered.

There wasn't a dry eye on that field.

Not even Jerry's.

After the Game

Back in the box, Carter fell asleep in his mother's arms, smiling.

Jerry came over quietly. "You know, I've signed a lot of big contracts. But that check today — that one means the most."

Mulligan nodded. "I'd offer you an autograph, sir, but my paw cramps."

Jerry laughed. "You're welcome here anytime, son."

Before we left, he pulled me aside.

"Cole, thank you for sharing those dogs with the world. They remind people what this game's really about."

On the drive home, the stadium lights faded in the rearview mirror. Mulligan stared out the window.

"Are you okay?" I asked.

He nodded. "We helped a kid forget about hospitals for a day. That's better than any trophy."

Georgette sighed. "And the lighting was perfect."

I laughed. "Only you could turn a miracle into a fashion statement."

Mulligan leaned over. "She's not wrong. We looked good out there."

I smiled, the warmth settling in — laughter, tears, grace, and one small boy's wish that reminded us why any of this matters.

"Boss," Mulligan said quietly, "you think Jerry would let me call a few plays next time?"

"Not a chance," I said.

"Good," he replied. "That team's stressful enough."

We rode the rest of the way home in silence, highway humming beneath us, Mulligan's head resting on my shoulder.

For once, he didn't have a punchline.

Just a sigh.

And a miracle still shining in his eyes.

Chapter 27 — The Blessing of the Beasts (and Everything Else)

The Call from Father Ben

It was a quiet Wednesday afternoon when my brother, Father Ben, called.

"Cole," he said, "I saw you on TV at that Cowboys game. You, the fancy poodle, and that mutt with the attitude — you're practically saints now."

I laughed. "We sanctified the end zone. Jerry said he's never seen so much prayer during a first down."

Ben chuckled. "Well, if you're finished evangelizing America's Team, I've got a new mission for you. St. Timothy's is hosting our annual Blessing of the Animals next weekend, and I want you, Mulligan, Georgette — and the whole crew — to be part of it."

"The whole crew?" I asked.

"Yes. Julia, her mother, Fa, and those little furballs, Anna Belle and Teddy. The more the merrier — or holier."

I hesitated. "Ben, you realize if we bring all of them, we're one hamster short of Noah's Ark."

"Perfect, St. Francis would approve."

Once word got out that Mulligan and Georgette would be appearing at St. Timothy's, the phones started ringing off the hook.

By Thursday, the church secretary sounded near tears.

"Father Ben," she said, "we've got everything from cats to cows registered. Someone just called asking if they can bring a ferret dressed as the Virgin Mary."

Mulligan perked up. "That's commitment."

Georgette arched her neck.

Anna Belle and Teddy barked in harmony, tails wagging as if they'd just been cast in a Disney movie.

Julia smiled. "Well, if this doesn't make the paper, nothing will."

Dane nodded calmly.

Fa said what we were all thinking. "Lord help us. Literally."

Sunday morning dawned bright — and loud. Too loud.

The church parking lot looked like the Fort Worth Zoo had thrown a parade. Dogs. Cats. Goats. Birds. Lizards. One pot-bellied pig in a tutu. And something that might've been a raccoon but arrived with paperwork.

Father Ben moved through the crowd in full vestments, aspergillum in hand, sprinkling holy water like a pro.

"Peace be with you," he said.

"And also with your fleas," Mulligan muttered.

Julia stood beside me, arm linked through mine, smiling like a proud mother at graduation.

Dane filmed everything.

Fa directed traffic with military precision, waving people forward like she was guiding planes on a runway.

Anna Belle and Teddy wore matching bow ties and posed for photos.

Georgette, naturally, wore a silk scarf embroidered with tiny gold crosses — a gift from a parishioner who'd discovered her online.

When Father Ben saw the crowd stretching down the block, he leaned over and whispered, "Cole, I think we've outgrown the ark."

The Sermon According to Mulligan

At ten-thirty sharp, Ben tapped the microphone.

"Friends, before we begin the blessing, I'd like to welcome our special guests — Cole Sheridan, Julia, Fa, Dane, and their four-legged ministers: Mulligan, Georgette, Anna Belle, and Teddy."

The applause was deafening — mostly from the dogs.

Mulligan strutted forward, tail high. "Thank you, thank you. Please, no autographs during Mass."

The crowd roared. Even Father Ben cracked a smile.

Then Mulligan grew serious — or as serious as Mulligan ever gets.

"I'm not a priest," he said, "though I did ask for one of those collars. Father Ben said it would be sacrilegious. Personally, I think it would've been stylish. But I do know this: dogs, cats, people — we're all made from the same breath. We wag, we weep, we forgive faster than we should. And if you ask me, that's proof enough that God's still in the creation business."

The crowd went still.

Even the parrot in the back whispered, "Amen."

Father Ben rested his hand on Mulligan's head. "That'll preach."

Mulligan grinned. "Good. I'll expect a tithe in treats."

Holy Water and Holy Chaos

Then came the blessing.

Father Ben dipped the aspergillum and began sprinkling holy water over the crowd.

Dogs barked in chorus. Cats yowled in protest. A Saint Bernard shook himself so hard he baptized everyone within ten feet.

The goat, startled, broke loose and ran straight for the altar.

Fa took off after it, yelling, "Somebody grab the holy goat!"

Julia laughed so hard she had to lean on me. Dane streamed the entire disaster live.

Anna Belle and Teddy stayed close to Georgette, who somehow remained elegant through it all — even as a parakeet landed on her head.

Father Ben stood there, drenched but smiling. "Every year, I pray for more joy. God really overdelivered."

After the Amen

By the end, everyone was soaked, smiling, and peaceful — humans and animals alike.

Father Ben addressed the crowd one last time.

"May your homes be full of life, your hearts full of compassion, and your carpets… miraculously stain resistant."

Laughter rippled through the crowd.

Mulligan leaned toward me. "That's one blessing I could use."

"Same," I said.

We posed for photos — the whole family, Father Ben in the center, surrounded by fur, feathers, and friends.

For one shining moment, everything felt exactly as it should.

On the drive home, the car smelled like holy water, wet dog, and joy.

Julia rested her head on my shoulder. "That was wonderful," she said.

"It really was," I replied. "I think Ben just got himself a viral video."

From the back seat, Mulligan yawned. "You know, Boss, for a guy without a collar, I'm feeling pretty blessed."

Anna Belle barked. Teddy wagged.

Georgette sighed contentedly. "Faith, family, and good grooming — that's heaven enough for me."

I smiled at the road ahead, heart full.

"Amen to that," I said.

And somewhere in the back seat, Mulligan whispered, "Next year, I'm bringing the ferret."

Chapter 28 — Back to Santa Anna

A week after Father Ben's Blessing of the Beasts, I told Mulligan we were heading to the ranch.

"You've heard me talk about it," I said. "Julia's mom and daddy's place outside Santa Anna. It's where Charlie roamed, where the sunsets stretch clear to heaven, and where this whole wild journey kind of started."

Mulligan's ears perked. "A ranch? Real cows?"

"Real cows," I said. "And a few heifers who think they own the place."

He grinned. "Boss, this is going to be my Yellowstone moment."

I told him Julia's fiftieth high school reunion was that weekend, and it was time for him and Georgette to see where it all began.

"I've got to go pick up the van," I said.

"Your van?"

"Our van," I corrected. "Technically, it doubles as a funeral-home family car, but mostly it's my travel loophole. I take out the front captain's seats — now we've got room for dog beds, water bowls, and enough space for your ego."

He nodded approvingly. "Does it have Wi-Fi?"

"Better," I said. "A TV and DVD player."

Mulligan's eyes widened. "Movie night in a van, driving to Santa Anna. Who would've thought?"

When I rolled back up the drive, Julia had packed half the pantry, and Dane had a loaded cooler. The dogs danced around the van like we were loading Noah's Ark.

"Everybody ready?" I asked.

Julia smiled. "As we'll ever be."

We hit the highway — Julia, Dane, Anna Belle, Teddy, Georgette, and Mulligan — me behind the wheel, king of the caravan.

Mulligan chose 101 Dalmatians for the first leg of the trip and split his time between the back bench and the front seat, offering running commentary.

Halfway to Dublin, he leaned forward. "Boss, are we going through that Dr Pepper place you told me about?"

"You bet. Dublin. Oldest bottler of Dr Pepper in Texas."

"Can we stop and get one like Charlie used to?"

"Of course," I said. "But fair warning — the big Dr Pepper folks and Dublin had a falling-out years ago. They don't call it Dr Pepper anymore, but the Dublin Bottling Works still makes soda with real cane sugar."

He frowned. "Soda?"

I laughed. "I know. Sounds like a Yankee word. Back home, every carbonated drink was a Coke. You just had to say what kind — Dr Pepper Coke, Sprite Coke, root beer Coke."

We pulled up to the old bottling plant, bought a case of Dublin Founders Recipe, four cups, and toasted Charlie.

Mulligan licked the rim. "Tastes like nostalgia and caffeine."

By late afternoon, we rolled through Santa Anna — a small town with a few hundred souls and a whole lot of memory. The water tower still leaned a little. The feed store still wore its faded 1950s Coke sign.

When we turned up the dirt road to the ranch, a big black bull watched us from behind the fence, surrounded by twenty-five heifers.

Dane's eyes glistened. You could see the homecoming written all over her face.

Inside, Julia immediately began her scorpion inspection, broom in hand like a samurai.

"Still dead," I called from across the room.

"Good," she said. "Let's keep it that way."

I leaned down to Mulligan and Georgette. "If you see one moving, don't play with it. The sting will set you free — not in a good way."

They nodded gravely.

The next morning, Julia and Dane wanted to take flowers to the cemetery — Burl's grave, her little brother's, and her grandparents.'

We loaded the flowers and dogs into the van and drove the winding lane lined with mesquites and bluebonnets.

At the gate, the air went still. Julia knelt, arranging the flowers just so, whispering memories into the wind.

Mulligan and Georgette stood quietly beside her. Even Teddy stayed still.

When she finished, Julia smiled. "Daddy would've loved you," she told Mulligan.

He blinked. "From what I've heard, ma'am, the feeling's mutual."

Afterward, we drove through town — her old high school, the soda shop that once served root beer floats, and the single-screen movie theater that hadn't shown a film since Reagan was president.

Each stop opened another story — pep rallies, homecoming mums, first dates, and the dance where Burl asked Dane to marry him.

Mulligan listened, spellbound. "Boss, this town's got more heart than Dallas and Fort Worth combined."

He wasn't wrong.

Steak, Stars, and Crickets

That evening, I fired up the grill as the sun dipped behind the ridge. The cows offered their evening gossip. Crickets tuned up. Somewhere far off, a coyote voiced his two-note opinion.

Mulligan sat on the porch steps, staring upward. "Boss," He whispered, "I've never seen so many stars."

"Out here," I said, "you realize how big heaven really is."

Inside, Julia and Dane laughed in the kitchen. Anna Belle claimed her spot beside Julia's chair. Teddy patrolled the hallway, chasing tennis balls I rolled down the long wood floor until Anna Belle decided sleep was the smarter sport.

When the steaks were gone and the dishes stacked, I lit a fire in the big stone fireplace.

We just sat — no TV, no noise — just flame, breath, and belonging.

Mulligan broke the silence. "Boss, this beats Netflix."

"Yep," I said. "That's the original streaming service — firelight."

The next morning, we took the Mule out for a ride. Mulligan rode shotgun, ears flapping, joy unfiltered.

Julia guided us down to the little pet cemetery near the creek. She brought wreaths for Lady, Ginger, Charlie, and all the others who'd shared this land with her.

Mulligan stood still as she placed each one. "Boss," he said quietly, "you folks sure know how to love."

"Yeah," I said. "And we don't forget easily."

The rest of the week drifted by — porch talks, morning coffee, cedar-scented air, and stories that didn't need endings.

I took Julia to her reunion Saturday night. She came home smiling, saying half her class looked great and the other half looked "highly accomplished in grandparenting."

While we were gone, Dane had the best caretakers in Texas — Mulligan, Georgette, Anna Belle, and Teddy — who apparently hosted a slumber party complete with paw prints on the guest bed.

On the drive home, Mulligan suggested another dog movie.

"Homeward Bound, seems fitting."

Julia and Dane opted for their soap opera instead.

So, Mulligan climbed into the front seat beside me, watching the road unspool west to east.

"Boss, you ever notice the best trips aren't really vacations? They're reminders of who we are."

I nodded. "You've been listening to Julia again."

He smiled. "Maybe. Or maybe I drank too much cane sugar in Dublin."

We rode the rest of the way in that comfortable silence only full hearts know.

When the ranch disappeared in the rearview mirror, Mulligan sighed.

"Boss?"

"Yeah?"

"Next time we go back, can we invite the stars too?"

"They'll be waiting," I said.

Chapter 29 — Back Among the Living

Morning Coffee at Guy Sheridan

A few days after returning from Santa Anna, Cole pulls into Guy Sheridan Funeral Home early, just as the sun is rising over the stone façade.

The parking lot smells faintly of rain and polished oak — that unmistakable scent of reverence and routine. Inside, Fa's already got coffee brewing, and Martha's setting up the register book for the day's visitation.

Mulligan trots in ahead of me, head high, tail wagging like he owns stock in the place.

"Smells like home."

"Yep," I tell him. "That's the smell of fifty years of people trusting us with what matters most."

We make the morning rounds — check the chapel lights, peek in the prep room (Mulligan refuses to go in, muttering something about "respect for the departed"), and greet the staff as they drift in.

Larry's first. "Morning, Boss," balancing his coffee and a powdered donut.

Mulligan eyes the donut. "You're not on fetch duty again, are you?"

Larry laughs. "Not today. The launcher's still cooling down from last time."

Even Georgette trots in from the family lounge with Julia, looking like she is visiting royalty.

"This place could use more fresh flowers," she remarks, nose in the air.

Fa smirks. "And less dog hair."

It feels good to laugh here again.

Across Town — Cole Sheridan & Son

By midmorning, we head across town to the second home — Cole Sheridan & Son Funeral Home — the younger, leaner one, all bright light and modern edges.

Jon's already there, meeting with a family. Brittany's rearranging floral tributes, and Peyton's at the desk, Cole the service dog napping beside her feet.

"Welcome back," Jon says, grinning. "We survived without you, but just barely."

"I can tell," I say, looking around at a spotless lobby. "The place looks too clean. Y'all have been slacking on personality."

Mulligan trots forward to inspect the floor, sniffing. "Efficient. Modern. But lacking in peanut butter treats."

When Jon finishes with the family, he joins me in the chapel. It's quiet there — the hum of air-conditioning, the smell of fresh lilies.

"This place," I tell him, "Is what I always hoped for — one built with love, but not afraid of change. We've come a long way from the hardwood floors and ceiling fans."

Jon nods. "And a long way from $20 dogs."

Mulligan winks. "Speak for yourself, kid. I'm still priceless."

We gather in the break room for lunch — the whole crew from both locations: Fa, Julia, Jon, Brittany, Peyton, and the dogs all at our feet.

Someone brings out sandwiches, someone else makes a toast with sweet tea.

I look around that table and think how many years are sitting there — laughter, funerals, storms, rebuilds, and small miracles.

"We've buried friends, heroes, strangers, and saints," I tell them. "And somehow, every one of them teaches us something —

how to live, how to forgive, how to keep showing up. This place is more than walls. It's holy ground — because love has walked through it."

Mulligan leans against my leg and says softly, "Boss, I think you're finally catching on."

Everyone laughs, but they know what he means.

That evening, I walked through each chapel, lights low, quiet as a prayer.

I stop at the front, where flowers from the day's service still linger, and whisper, "Thank you" — to the room, the work, and every soul who's trusted us to tell their story right.

Outside, Mulligan sits on the curb beside me, watching the streetlights flicker on.

"Good day?" I ask.

He nods. "The best. You brought the story home."

I smile. "Guess we both did."

"Yeah," he says, stretching. "Now let's go start the credits."

Chapter 30 — After the Storm

(Twenty Dollars Well Spent)

Dinner dishes clinked softly in the sink, the smell of roast and cornbread still hanging in the air.

Outside, a front was rolling in — that big-sky Texas kind of night, when the horizon turns lavender and the clouds look like they're taking attendance before a storm.

Inside, we were settling in for movie night.

The fire was lit, logs popping and crackling like an old friend clearing his throat before telling a good story.

Anna Belle trotted in carrying the unopened bag of popcorn — her usual hint that it was time for family.

Julia sat curled on the couch with Anna Belle tucked against her side, the way they've done for years. Dane was in her favorite chair, Georgette draped elegantly across her lap like a living fur stole. Teddy sat beside me, leaning his warm shoulder into my leg, sighing like he'd officially clocked out for the night.

Mulligan and Georgette claimed the rug in front of the fireplace — front-row seats for whatever we watched… or didn't.

"Boss," Mulligan said, "may I suggest a classic?"

I grinned. "Sure. What's the pick?"

"Marley & Me."

Julia groaned. "Oh no. Not that one again. We can't handle another ugly cry."

Mulligan shrugged. "Fine. Turner & Hooch."

Teddy thumped his tail with approval.

I hit play. The opening credits rolled, and for a moment everything felt perfectly still — the kind of still you wish you could bottle.

Halfway through the movie, thunder grumbled across the sky. The windows rattled, the fire hissed — and then click — darkness.

The house went quiet except for the wind and the slow percussion of rain on the roof.

For a few seconds, nobody moved.

Then Julia said softly, "Well… there goes movie night."

Mulligan stretched, eyes glowing in the firelight. "Maybe this is the sequel," he said. "Talking Dog $20 — The Blackout Chronicles."

We laughed. And when the laughter faded, it gave way to that easy silence that only comes when you're exactly where you're supposed to be.

The storm rolled on. Lightning flashed across the windows, each burst lighting the room like a memory:

Sunny at the golf course, laughing through the wind.
Father Ben sprinkling holy water over a runaway goat.
Carter at the Cowboys game, smiling bigger than Texas itself.
Julia and Dane at the ranch, wreaths in hand, whispering love into the past.
Clint and the kids chasing lightning bugs in the yard, my grandson shouting that this was "the best night of his life."

The renewed joy inside both funeral homes — families laughing through tears, our staff living the ministry instead of just the work.
Children at the hospital hugging our dogs like they were hope itself.
Mothers and little ones at the night shelter, faces softening when Mulligan lay his head in their laps.
Hospice nurses smiling gently.
Peaceful eyes of those ready to cross over.

The choir at St. Timothy's, voices rising like they might out-sing grief.

Each flash was a note in a hymn God had been writing all along — a song of laughter, service, and grace that somehow carried my name in the harmony.

The thunder eased. Rain still whispered against the windows, but the room had gone utterly still — no TV glow, no chatter, just the soft breathing of everyone I loved.

Julia slept on the couch with Anna Belle tucked tight against her side.
Across the room, Dane sat in her chair, Georgette curled like a white cloud in her lap.
Teddy leaned heavily and warmly against my leg.
Mulligan and Georgette lay on the rug in front of the fire, paws touching, eyes half-closed.

I looked around that room — the whole mismatched family God had stitched together out of laughter, loss, and second chances — and thought:

If heaven needs a waiting room, I hope it looks like this.

"Boss," Mulligan murmured without opening his eyes.

"Yeah, buddy?"

"You ever think about how all this started?"

"All the time," I said. "A crooked sign. Twenty bucks. One talking dog."

He smiled, feeling sleepy but satisfied. "Best investment you've ever made."

The fire cracked softly.

"You know, Mulligan," I said after a while, "I've preached comfort all my life and helped families say goodbye. And tell them to have faith. But I don't think I really understood grace until you showed up."

He opened one eye.
"Grace isn't something you understand, Boss." It's something you bump into."

Thunder rumbled far off — more benediction than warning.

I whispered, "You think this was a God thing?"

Mulligan's tail thumped once.
"Boss," everything good is a God thing. You just needed a dog to point it out."

The fire dimmed to embers. Peace settled over us like a quilt.

I scratched Teddy's ears. He sighed, content.

Mulligan lifted his head and looked at me the way only he can. "Get some rest, tomorrow's another story."

I smiled. "You're right, partner. But tonight, I think I'll listen."

I leaned back, watching the last coal fade to red, and for the first time in a long while, I didn't feel the need to ask for anything — because I already knew.

Sometimes God doesn't speak in thunder.
Sometimes he whispers through laughter, through loss, through a twenty -dollar dog who won't stop talking.

And in that whisper, you know.

And that knowing…
is enough.

End of Book

Acknowledgments

Writing this book has been one of the most joyful adventures of my life.

To **Janice (Julia),** my compass, my calm, and the one who laughs at the same stories no matter how many times she's heard them.

To **Jon (Clint)** for building on the legacy with kindness, integrity, and heart.

To **Myrl and Fawn (Burl and Dane),** the greatest mother and father-in-law anyone could ever ask for. Your love, strength, and quiet wisdom have shaped our family more than you'll ever know.

To **Father Tim (Father Ben)** for reminding me that faith and humor are siblings, not strangers, and that grace often arrives smiling.

To **Martha (Fa)** for always being there, for standing beside me through everything, and for being a twin in every way that matters.

To everyone at **Thompson's Harveson & Cole Funeral Home** and **Martin Thompson & Son Funeral Home** — thank you for living the ministry, not just doing the work. You honor this calling every day.

To my friends who pushed, polished, challenged, and encouraged this project — you know who you are, and I'm deeply grateful.

And finally, to every family who has ever trusted us with their loved one's story: you taught me that every goodbye deserves dignity, compassion, a touch of laughter, and a whole lot of love.

About the Author

Martin Thompson is a second-generation funeral director and storyteller based in Fort Worth, Texas. For more than five decades, he has helped families celebrate lives with equal parts reverence, compassion, and laughter.

He owns and operates **Thompson's Harveson & Cole Funeral Home** and **Martin Thompson & Son Funeral Home** alongside his son, Jon, continuing a family legacy of service that spans more than a century.

When he isn't helping families or writing, Martin can usually be found on the golf course, watching TCU Horned Frogs football, or relaxing at home with his wife Janice, their family, and an ever-growing pack of loyal dogs.

The Mulligan Chronicles: Second Chances — A Story of Loss, Faith, and Redemption is his fourth book, following *Funeral Begins with Fun, Heart and Humanity: A Funeral Director's Chronicle of the World's Oldest Calling*, and *The Mulligan Chronicles: Talking Dog $20 — A Texas Tale*.

Martin believes every good story — especially one involving a talking dog — is proof that God still works through humor, heart, and the occasional wagging tail.

www.ingramcontent.com/pod-product-compliance
Lightning Source LLC
LaVergne TN
LVHW020418070526
838199LV00055B/3658